# HUNTER FROM THE RIFT

## LEE BEZOTTE

INSPARKET
MEDIA

Insparket Media
P.O. Box 1654
Moline, IL 61266

www.insparket.com

ISBN: 978-0-9976915-6-6
eISBN: 978-0-9976915-7-3

This book is dedicated to all who stubbornly refuse to let others suffer.

## CHAPTER ONE

# AN UNPLEASANT
# HOLIDAY

F aymia was filled with equal parts expectation and
preoccupation as she rode east atop her horse,
Addoe. The rhythmic thud of the animal's hooves
against the road and the repetitive rocking she experienced
as it trotted along were making her feel drowsy. "We should
be at the outer edges of it by supper," she announced,
answering her companion's repeated question for the
twenty-third time.

Maren sat sleepily behind her, resting the side of her
face against Faymia's back. She wore an eye patch because
she so admired the one Faymia wore. It was one that Son
had made for her a while back. However, she claimed that
the piece of leather was making her face sweaty and had
twisted it so that it had become more of an ear patch.
"Ohdium Rift," she whispered to herself. "What are we
going to do there?"

The woman took a deep breath, preparing herself to
answer another repeated question with grace and patience.
"I was born there, but my mother moved us away while I

was still a babe. I have no memory of the place. I hear it's beautiful, so I thought it would be a nice place to visit while Dulnear and Son are away in the north."

Maren adjusted the eye patch once more, sliding it around so that it now looked like a headband. Rubbing her ear where the patch once rested, she asked, "When will they come back?"

"At the..." Faymia began to answer but was pulled from her thought. She noticed a caravan and several men on horseback blocking the road up ahead. Seeing anyone but the occasional farmer along this road was unusual, so the sight made her uneasy. She slowed down to survey their surroundings for a way to bypass them. Pushed up against the north side of the road were rock walls topped with jagged stone fingers. They ran as far down the trail as she could see. The southern edge of the road dropped off into a rolling creek. If she tried to avoid the blockade, she would not be able to do so by casually veering off the road.

Her young passenger peered around her and inquired, "Who are they?"

"Possibly a dubious toll set up by local drunkards. Hopefully, they'll just ask for a copper and wave us on through," the woman said, though she felt less than certain about her answer.

Maren tilted her head sideways and asked, "If the toll isn't supposed to be there, then why should we pay it?"

"Because it's better than fighting half a dozen booze-hounds for passage east," Faymia answered. "Now, sit up straight, pay close attention to them, and keep your hand near your sword in case you need it." She then took several slow, deep breaths as they approached the group closing off the road.

"Why would I need my sword?" Maren asked.

"Shhhh," she sibilated. "No more talking until we're through."

As they drew near, Faymia could feel Maren's hands gripping ever more tightly at her sides and a slight tremble ran through them. The smell of gaudy cologne began to fill her nostrils and she immediately recognized the men as slavers.

The caravan obstructed most of the road from north to south. A man sat atop his horse facing westward while another man stood on the south side of the road with a bottle dangling from his right hand. The other men were scattered along the narrow surface between the road and the creek.

"Whoa!" the westward-facing man called out from atop his steed. He was older, dark-skinned, and disheveled yet dapper-looking. He wore a fine coat that fell below his knees, but something about his appearance was akin to a farm animal that had been dressed by an expensive tailor.

Faymia halted Addoe. A drop of sweat ran down her side and she began to wonder if a holiday away was such a good idea. Her previous experience as a slave made her particularly uncomfortable around the unsavory lot, and she did her best to maintain a cool composure. "Is this a toll?" she asked, pretending to smile politely.

"Maybe," the bottle-wielding man belched out from the road to the right of her. The whiskery toad was also dressed in fine clothing, but appeared as if he hadn't washed in a while.

The woman could feel the young girl behind her grasp even tighter with her right hand and reach up to massage her ear with her left hand. Breathing slowly and deliberately, Faymia gave her a reassuring pat on the leg while courteously asking the man on horseback, "How much do I owe you, good sir?"

"I'll take the eye patch," the man in the road said with a phlegmy laugh that was followed by a hacking cough.

Faymia suppressed a look of disgust toward him. Their attire made them look out of place in the rugged farmland, and she would rather endure the stench of manure than continue to smell their strong cologne. She imagined the caravan to be stocked with more booze than food. Her disdain of their lot was an ever-growing source of indignation for her. As she slowly moved her hand closer to the hilt of her sword, she shot, "Excuse me?"

"Take it off!" he came back, reaching for her horse's rein.

"Leave her alone!" the other man yelled from atop his horse. "They're not the ones we're looking for."

The drunkard curled his lip, dropped the rein, and took a step backward. "I was just having some fun," he mumbled before taking another swig.

"You can go," the other slaver deadpanned as he waved them on.

Faymia nodded, then turned her gaze forward. She brought Addoe to a trot and moved through the blockade without making eye contact with the other men littered along the side of the road. When they were a comfortable distance east of the group, she could feel Maren's grip relax and the tension in her own shoulders began to dissipate. "Are you feeling better?" she asked the girl.

"Uh-huh," Maren answered unconvincingly, then twisted the eye patch around to cover her left eye once more.

"Well, hopefully Son and Dulnear are having a better time than this," Faymia sighed as she urged Addoe to move just a little faster.

>>>————•————→

"It's freezing!" Son complained. "Why are we training without our coats?" he asked as his wild, blond hair blew across his face.

"Focus!" Dulnear said in a low, commanding voice. As he brought his sword down toward the boy's left shoulder, he continued. "You must control your body instead of allowing the conditions around you to dictate your attention. Discomfort will teach you during this season of learning."

The two had built a makeshift training camp on a high shelf protruding from the southern side of one of the Petraig Mountains. Trees grew around the edges of the shelf and its floor was covered with sparse, patchy grass and pine needles.

The sky was harsh and cold, and the dense clouds surrounding the mountain made it difficult to see. Son was looking forward to taking a break and warming himself by the fire but that luxury didn't seem to be coming anytime soon.

The boy quickly shifted his posture and blocked his

mentor's sword. "I can barely see," he continued his grievance.

"Then use your ears," the man from the north instructed with a hint of annoyance in his voice. "Or your sense of touch. How does the air feel against your skin when a sword passes by?" He then swung his blade toward the boy's neck, which was blocked skillfully. "And what about your sense of smell?" he added. "Learn to use these and you will always have the upper hand against a violent brute swinging wildly."

"Well, I can definitely smell you," Son needled before rolling past his friend and slapping his sword against the giant man's backside.

Dulnear growled and spun around to face the boy. However, his gruff demeanor soon passed and he began to laugh. "Right on the doleum!" he exclaimed, rubbing his bottom. Giving a conceding nod, he sheathed his sword and tilted his head toward their shelter. "Let us sit by the fire for a moment."

As the two walked across the cloudy ledge, Son heard an animal cry out in the unseen distance, unearthing a fear he much wished to keep buried. It sent a shiver through his neck and he quickened his pace toward the fire. "What do you think is going to happen?" he asked as he sat down and began rubbing his hands together. He had placed logs along the ground for him and Dulnear to sit on. However, they were quickly disappearing as they were needed for firewood.

"Happen with what?" his friend asked.

"Ocmallum knows where we live," the boy explained. "Do you think he'll come after us?"

"I do not know," the northerner confessed. "However,

we are here in Tuas-arum, Faymia and Maren are on holiday, and there is not a slaver in sight. Keep your focus on this time of training where it belongs."

"But shouldn't we be digging a moat around the farm, or setting traps or something?" the boy fretted.

Dulnear let out an amused chuckle at the question. Picking at the fire with a stick in his left hand, he asked, "When is the best time to build a cottage?"

Son wasn't expecting a question like that, and he was agitated by the warrior's apparent complacency concerning their looming threat. "I don't know. As soon as you purchase the land, I suppose."

"Yes," Dulnear said. "That is true. One does not wait until it rains or snows to build." Repeating the question, he asked, "So, when is the best time to build a cottage?"

Staring across the fire at his friend, Son took a deep breath. Then, it struck him. "Before you need it!" he shouted.

"That is correct," the northerner acknowledged. "We do not know what is coming. There is no way for us to be certain. The only things we can be certain of are those things that are within our power to control. And right now, it is within our power to make you a more skilled warrior."

"But I'm already a pretty skilled warrior, don't you think?" the boy asked with a cocky smile. "I mean, I smacked you on the doleum, or whatever you called it."

"That you did," the man replied. "But when I am training you, I hold back so that you can learn, and so that I do not hurt you." He then added with a grin, "And I don't think smacks on the bottom will be enough to stop slaver mercenaries."

Son couldn't help but wonder now if he was actually growing in his skills, or if his teacher was merely bolstering his confidence. "Hold back?" he yelped. "Why don't you let me fight you fairly?"

"I am letting you fight me fairly," Dulnear chuckled. "It would be very unfair for me to not exercise restraint with you."

"But I fought Searfain and did well," the boy declared.

"Yes, but Searfain was a drunken brute," the man from the north stated. "And besides, you had Faymia's help."

Son pursed his lips and released a long sigh through his nostrils. Now that he was nearing manhood, he felt the need to express his ability to handle himself. Finally, he suggested, "How about we spar once without restraint?"

The warrior's head went back and he rubbed his forehead just above his strong brow. "I do not think you know what you are asking," he cautioned.

"I'll be fine," the boy assured.

"I would feel horrible if I hurt you," the man worried.

"You won't," Son said as he stood up from his log. "Here, we'll use wood instead of swords." He then grabbed a couple of nearby sticks from the ground and tossed one to Dulnear, goading, "Come on, just once. I promise not to hit your bum again."

The large man sighed and stood to his feet. "Well, if you insist," he said as he adjusted his grip on the branch with his left hand. "But let us move away from this fire first. I would not want to fall into it if you knocked me down."

"Good idea," the boy agreed as he stepped back into the open area of the shelf. Taking a ready stance, he clutched his makeshift sword with a steel grip. "Ready?" he asked, breathing in quick, deep breaths.

"I am ready," Dulnear said as he drew closer and leaned his shoulders slightly toward the boy.

Son took a deep breath, looked intently into his friend's eyes, and prompted, "Begin!"

He barely noticed his friend's wrist twitch when he felt a painful strike to the side of his head. Darkness quickly crept over his eyes and he fell to the ground unconscious.

CHAPTER TWO

# THE OHDIUM
# RIFT

"It's over there," Faymia announced as she pointed toward a distant ravine. A growing fog in the air made it difficult to see, but the woman's keen eye immediately spotted the interruption in the somewhat monotonous landscape. It seamlessly blended in with its surroundings, much like a derelict castle does when it has been overtaken by years of moss and ivy. The Rift began a stone's throw from the road and ran south as far as she could see.

Maren pulled her hand from her ear and used her arms to hold Faymia's shoulders in an attempt to prop herself up for a better view. "Where?" she asked with fresh energy.

"There," the woman said, hoping that if she said it louder and pointed more aggressively, the young girl would see it.

Maren squinted and tilted her head. "I kind of see it."

"That's understandable. Many people ride right by it every day without realizing what they are passing."

As they drew closer, a lightness filled Faymia's chest.

There was something whimsical about visiting the place of her birth for the first time. She veered off the road and onto a trail that led steadily downward. As they carefully descended, mossy cliffs began to rise to the east of them. To the other side of them, the ground rolled gradually westward. Its hills and leveled surfaces were covered in dense forest. Occasionally, one of them would spot another trail veering into the forest or up the steep slope leading toward the cliffs, but they continued south, deeper in.

Eventually, Maren began to let loose an occasional, "Hey there," from behind her friend. "Ho," she said, immediately turning her right ear toward the space where her mouth just was. "Hello," she said again, quickly swiveling her head. "The air is strange here," she noted.

"I suppose it is," Faymia admitted as she swiped her finger over an itch that lingered beneath the patch covering her left eye. "There's no breeze, and it feels extra damp."

They continued their trek a little further until they reached the bottom of the ravine and the ground leveled and began to open up. "Look up there," Maren said, pointing toward the cliffs to the east.

"Up where?"

"Where I'm pointing," the girl explained with irritation in her voice.

The woman paused for a moment, then answered, "You're riding behind me, so I can't see where you're pointing. What would you like me to see?"

"There are houses carved into those cliffs!" Maren exclaimed.

Faymia quickly craned her neck upward and gazed at the cliffs. There were what appeared to be dwellings carved within the cliff wall. They were covered completely by foliage, and blended well with their surroundings. Halting her horse, she observed, "Isn't that interesting. Do you want to get a closer look?"

"Umm...yes," Maren said with hesitation.

"I'm sure it'll be fine," the woman assured, and she rode as close to the cliff as she could before tying Addoe to a tree and continuing on foot.

"How will we get up there?" her young companion asked.

"I'm sure there's a way," Faymia assured. "There has to be, right?"

"I guess so," Maren answered, now massaging her ear.

Faymia withdrew her sword and hacked away at some of the ivy along the foot of the cliff, and did her best to pull it away from the wall.

Emulating her friend, the young girl slid the leather patch back over her eye, withdrew her sword, and began cutting vines along the ground and pulling them away from the cliff. Shuffling through the chopped, creeping vegetation, she saw something. "What's this?" she asked.

Faymia went to where Maren was standing and helped her pull a few handfuls of vine away. Inspecting the wall where they stood, she observed, "Looks like hand and footholds carved into the stone."

"Are we supposed to climb up those?" the girl asked.

"Why not?" Faymia smiled.

"Because it looks like death," Maren fretted.

Faymia chuckled at the dramatic description of the stone ladder. "I think we'll be fine. We'll just explore a little and come right back down."

Maren sighed, "All right," and followed Faymia up the first few rungs.

The two carefully ascended the rocky ladder, occasionally looking down to survey the Rift from a new height. Reaching the top, they hefted themselves into the cliff dwelling.

"Well, that's quite the view, isn't it!" the woman exclaimed. A mist was settling into the ravine, and the deep greens of vegetation contrasted against the black rock of the cliff made for an inspiring picture. She looked up at the sky above and admired its beauty laying hard against their surroundings. Her admiration was broken suddenly when she heard her friend let out a shriek.

"Yuck!" the girl yelled. "Bats. And they keep pooping!"

Faymia spun around to face the inside of the abandoned home. Though the outward-facing walls had remnants of ornate carvings covered by moss, the inside very much resembled a cave. Though she could tell that it went far back, and there was space to explore, the crumbling walls, cobwebs, and bats made for a less-than-tempting offering. "It's all right," she assured her friend. "They won't hurt you. Besides, I don't think we'll be here long."

"Good," Maren chirped. "I thought you were going to want to spend the night here." She then went to the edge of the dwelling, faced out toward the Rift, and bellowed, "Hello! Hey-oh!"

"Back to that again, are you?" the woman asked.

"It's strange," the girl murmured.

"What's strange?"

"The sound. It's buttoned up," the girl explained. "Hubbub!" she then shouted out.

Faymia leaned her right ear further out of the opening, examining the characteristics of Maren's voice as it traveled through the air. "There's no echo," she noticed.

"It's like yelling into a blanket," Maren said loudly.

"I suppose it is," the woman agreed, wondering how often her little friend actually yelled into a blanket. She then picked up a loose stone from the floor of the dwelling and flung it out into the ravine. Taken aback by the quality of the sound its landing made, she asked, "Did you hear that?"

"Uh-huh."

"Dead as a doornail." The excitement of coming to the Rift began to wear off of Faymia as the eeriness of their surroundings became more evident. "I wonder," she added. "Where are all the people?"

Maren continued to make noises into the air. However, the noises grew much quieter and she returned to massaging her ear.

"I have an idea," the woman said. Visiting the Ohdium hadn't turned out as she expected it would, and spending the next few days in a dank ravine didn't seem like an enjoyable holiday.

"What's that?"

"How about we find a nice clearing on the other side of the Rift and set up camp for the night. Then, in the morning, we'll go back to the farm."

Maren's eyes lit up. "Yes!" she piped, and darted for the stone ladder.

Surprised by the girl's response, Faymia followed after her. "Well then, I guess we're done here," she said. The idea of spending a few days relaxing at home had a growing appeal to her, and she felt a growing happiness about their decision in her chest.

>>>————·————

Faymia lay on her back near the fire watching sparks of glowing ash float into the pitch-black night sky. Nearby, she could hear Maren breathing heavily in her sleep. For days, she had looked forward to this trip. She had planned on exploring the area with her young friend and experiencing new people and places. Now, she just wanted to be home, and she felt it was odd that she did. There was just something unsettling about the Rift to her. It was an elusive feeling that she hoped was simply hunger or fatigue masquerading as a sense of dread. The only reason she chose to camp there was that it provided ample coverage from the cold wind.

As her eyes grew heavy, she imagined being with her husband again, living in the cottage they built together on the southern edge of Gale Hill Farm. Just as she was passing into slumber, she thought she heard whispers in the forest surrounding their camp. Her initial impression was that it was a dream trying to penetrate her conscious thoughts, but then she heard it again.

Placing her hand on the hilt of her sword, she continued to lay still. "Maren," she whispered, hoping the girl would whisper in return. She lay there, frozen for a moment.

"Maren," she tried again.

She then slowly reached her free hand above her head

and felt along the ground for the girl. Finding her ear, she gently tugged on it. "Maren, wake up," she breathed.

"Don't," the young gurl muttered, then rolled onto her side.

"Get 'em!" Faymia heard someone shout before feeling a heavy rope net land over her.

"No!" she yelled, pulling at the rope, furiously trying to get out from underneath it.

Something struck her shoulder and she felt a sharp pain run down her arm. Then, a similar sensation filled the back of her head. That time, she realized that jagged rocks from the Rift floor were being thrown at her.

"Maren!" she shouted, and wrestled through the net to place her body over the girl's.

"What's happening?" Maren asked through groggy tears.

"I don't know," the woman said as another stone struck her side. Turning her head slightly toward the commotion, she called out, "Who are you? Why are you doing this?"

An angry voice replied, "You know why, uplander!" and more pain radiated through her left arm.

"Please!" was all Faymia could cry out before a strange sound, like a massive horn, filled the air and vibrated through her chest until it drowned out the howling attackers.

Suddenly, the pelting of stones stopped, but the woman continued to cover Maren in case it began again. "Everything's fine," she reassured the girl. "I have you."

"Show no mercy!" a voice boomed from somewhere in the darkness, and clashing of metal could be heard.

"Are you all right?" Faymia asked her friend through the ruckus.

"I'll be fine," the girl's quivering voice answered.

"I think we're caught in the middle of a feud of some sort."

"What? What do we do?"

"We need to get out of this net!" Faymia instructed, and the two of them began to lift sections of rope and push them over their shoulders.

Finally, with the fire to their backs and the sound of fighting dwindling, they crawled out from underneath their confinement. Beaten and bloodied, Faymia stood to her feet. It seemed that no one was paying any attention to them anymore. Scanning the barely lit area, she asked, "Where's Addoe?"

Grasping Faymia's hand tightly with one hand and pointing to a place nearby, Maren answered, "He was over there."

Faymia began to limp forward toward where her friend was pointing. She prayed that she would be able to find the animal before they were attacked again. Stumbling into the darkness, she felt a powerful hand grab her arm and a voice commanded, "Stop!"

Before she could turn around, she felt something being forced over her head. It had the familiar smell of burlap and it dragged her eye patch low over her face. Flailing and clawing to pull the sack off of her, she panicked as one being held under water.

Maren could be heard screaming nearby. "Get off of me!" she shrieked. She then made threats that would make the most hardened of men blush.

There was a sensation of being hefted onto a large shoulder, and Faymia felt herself being quickly carried away through the night air. It was difficult to gauge which direction she was being taken, and she carefully used her ears to listen for Maren.

## CHAPTER THREE

# THE RUHBREM

"Who are you?" Faymia heard someone yell. Through the burlap sack over her head, she saw waving orange light, and the questioning voice echoed off distant stone walls. *I'm in a large room lit by torches*, she thought to herself. *Where have they taken me, and why?*

Her wounds were aching, and the cold wooden chair she was tied to was doing little to make her more comfortable.

"Where is the girl?" she asked. "Is she unharmed?"

"That depends," another voice fumed. "Tell us who you are and what your plans are!"

The woman's concern for Maren began to fill her veins with intense heat. Unhappy with the man's answer, she pushed aside the pain, forced her body to sit up straight, and replied with a snarl, "I am Faymia, and my plans are to retrieve my friend! Who are you?"

"We'll do the questioning here!" the second voice barked. "What were you doing in the Neodrec?"

"Neodrec?" she answered. "I don't even know what that is. I thought I was in the Ohdium Rift."

"You ARE in the Ohdium," the first voice answered. "The Neodrec is the neutral ground between us high-grounders and those wretched lowground scum."

"I don't know what you're talking about!" Faymia exclaimed. "I'm just a visitor here on holiday."

"You're lying!" the second voice accused. "You're a spy from the other side!"

"I was caught in the middle of a confrontation!" she shouted. "And I'm pretty sure that I was assaulted from *both* sides!"

"Probably a setup!" the same man sneered. "You lowgrounders are so conniving."

"I'm no spy. I was born here but raised elsewhere. My mother told me about the Rift," she explained. Then she added, "Though she never said anything about high-grounders or lowgrounders, or a Neodrec."

"Then your mother is a liar too!" the voice barked again, then rushed closer.

"Wait a minute!" a new voice broke in. It was deeper, and carried an air of authority.

The room grew quiet and, for the first time, Faymia could hear the forcefulness of her heart beating in her chest. Squinting to see through the burlap, she could now make out the silhouettes of three men against moving torchlight.

"Remove the blindfold," the third voice ordered.

One of the other men grabbed the sack and roughly yanked it off her head. As he did, the wounds she received from her attackers began to throb anew. Glancing around the room, she could see that she was seated near a large, round table. Behind the table, the floor stood slightly higher and was adorned with a beautifully ornate throne that seemed to be carved out of the very stone the room was carved from.

"Where am I?" Faymia demanded.

"You are in my chamber," the third man answered as he slowly stepped toward her. He was older than the other two men, and his clothes looked more refined. His gray-and-black beard and swept-back hair gave him a regal appearance, yet his skin told of a man who had worked very hard with his hands. "My name is Thuaid, and I rule over the Ruhbrem, the eastern side of the Ohdium."

"I thought the Rift was abandoned," the woman said. "When we arrived, there was nothing but rubble."

"That part is abandoned," Thuaid explained. "We have settled further south where the neutral ground is broader and we don't have to deal with the lowgrounders as much. At least that was the case for a while."

"Then all of this is carved from the cliffs?" Faymia asked, gesturing with her chin.

The leader pointed toward the ropes around her hands and feet, and one of the other men rushed over to untie them. "Yes. Our entire village is situated in the rock facing west." He then took a chair from the large table, sat down facing her, and said, "You said you were born here. Who were your mother and father?"

"My mother's name was Maylia," she answered, then paused. "I'm afraid I don't know who my father was."

The two assistants glanced at one another, and one of them began to snicker.

"Is that amusing to you?" Faymia snapped. As she did,

she balled her hands into fists, quickly trying to restore circulation to them.

"Hush!" Thuaid commanded his underling. Then, directing his attention back to the woman, he said, "My apologies. Maylia was a common name here many years ago. There was a time when we were all one people. There was no Ruhbrem, and no Taalbrem. Only the Ohdium, and we all lived together peacefully. There were even structures in what is now the neutral zone. They were beautiful, but they've been torn down."

"What happened?" the woman asked.

The chief took a long breath as he fixed his eyes on the ceiling of the chamber. Exhaling, he answered, "Those living in the lowlands wanted more. They envied our way of life. They continually raised our cost to borrow lands from them to grow our crops. They even tried to usurp some of our cliff dwellings."

Faymia listened to the man as he lamented the state of his land. There were offenses upon offenses, and it was often difficult to track where one occurrence began and another ended. The tangled stories and confusing accounts made it difficult to focus on a thread she could follow for a significant amount of time. It was much like the stories Dulnear had told her about the north. Eventually, she decided to interrupt. "I'm sorry to seem insensitive, sir," she said with as much compassion as she could portray with her eyes. "But I would really like to know where my companion is."

"Oh, yes," the man said apologetically. "The girl is fine. She is in my kitchen having a pudding."

"A pudding?" Faymia sputtered.

"Yes. When she was questioned, she didn't seem to know much about anything, except maybe pirates. My maid took to her and gave her some sweets," Thuaid explained. He then ordered one of his assistants to bring the girl to them.

When the assistant returned with Maren, she ran to Faymia and threw her arms around her neck. "They gave me pudding!" the girl exclaimed.

Trying not to respond to the aches brought on by Maren's hug, the woman replied, "I'm so glad you're unhurt. Are you ready to go home?"

The Ruhbrem leader stood up and gave a slight bow. "Please, you're wounded and hungry, and it's very late. I would be honored if you enjoyed our hospitality for a few days so you can recover."

Faymia knew the man was right. It would be a very difficult journey home in the condition she was in, but something about these people made her uncomfortable. Hoping she was not making a mistake, she answered, "Very well, but for no longer than I need to. I would not want to make myself a burden."

"Excellent!" Thuaid said with a genuine smile. He then instructed his aides to lead their guests to a room and provide them with supplies so they could tend to their needs.

## CHAPTER FOUR

# ALL THAT IS WORTH KNOWING

Dulnear and Son sat across the fire from each other. As the northerner sipped his coffee, he watched the boy poke at the glowing embers with a stick. They hadn't said much to each other since the previous day, and it was important to the man that they resume their training. Spying the purplish, inflamed bruise along Son's cheek and temple, he winced and apologized, "Once again, I am deeply sorry for the injury."

Son released a deep breath, pursed his lips and admitted, "It's my fault. I told you not to hold back. It was a lesson in overconfidence. You don't need to keep apologizing."

"You are too gracious," the warrior said. "Do you feel well enough to continue training this morning?"

The boy reached up to assess the injury with his fingertips, grimacing as he gently touched it. "I suppose so. Does it look bad?"

Dulnear paused for a moment and tilted his head, answering, "Not at all." He then swallowed and added, "It already looks to be healing." He was glad to be sitting on the other side of the fire so the boy couldn't see his face turning flush from stretching the truth.

"Well then, I suppose," Son said as he stood up to retrieve his sword.

"You will not be needing that," the man from the north said, standing to his feet as well. "I think we should spend some time working on your empty-handed fighting skills."

The boy walked slowly into the center of the clearing atop the mountainside shelf. His shoulders hung limp, and his feet clung closely to the ground as he walked. He swept his hair out of his face and took a lackluster fighting stance toward his mentor. "Let's do this," he mumbled.

"It will be all right," Dulnear assured. "I promise not to hurt you."

Son relaxed his stance, glanced at the ground, and lamented, "It's not that. It's that we've been training for years and I don't feel like any more of a warrior than I was when we first met."

The man moved closer and put his hand on the boy's shoulder. "What does it mean to you to feel like a warrior?" he asked.

"I don't know," Son said. "More confident, I suppose."

"There are many confident fools and weaklings," the warrior offered. "And I have never met another lad as tenacious and willing to learn as you."

"I thought maybe I was growing," Son continued. "I even thought that my senses were becoming more attuned to my surroundings."

"How do you mean?" the man from the north asked.

"For days I have felt that someone was watching us. At

first I ignored it, because we're in such a faraway place, but the feeling won't go away." The boy then paused and looked around. "But we're clearly the only ones here, and I'm just full of fear."

Dulnear looked him in the eyes and gave him a crooked half-smile. "Interesting."

Son wrinkled his nose and squinted his eyes. "What's interesting?"

"You should trust your gut, boy," the man answered.

"Why?"

Dulnear leaned in a little closer and lowered his voice. "Because there *has* been someone watching us for days."

The boy's eyes grew wide and he threw his shoulders back. "Then I was right?"

"Yes. You were," his mentor answered.

"Then why aren't we going after them?" Son asked, beginning to walk back to the shelter for his sword.

The man from the north took hold of the boy's arm and calmly answered, "We do not know who they are, how many there are, or if they even have ill intent." He then surveyed the trees surrounding the shelf and added, "Besides, something tells me that if they were going to attack us, they would have done so by now."

"But, what if you're wrong?" Son pressed.

Dulnear knew that being wrong was a possibility. He did not want to worry the already anxious lad. Rubbing his chin, he answered, "Then together we shall make them wish they would have chosen a different mountain."

>>>———•———

"Maren!" Faymia cried out.

Panic filled her chest, and it felt as if the very darkness that surrounded her was lashing out. Her dream seemed so real that the hushed voice inside of her, the one that tried to tell her she was dreaming, couldn't be heard.

She dreamed she was in the neutral zone, still camped near the abandoned cliff dwellings. The wind had blown the fire out and she was frantically reaching for her young companion. The sound of growling wolves drew nearer and fear wrapped itself around her, constricting her lungs.

"Maren!" she cried out again. "Where are you?"

The urge to draw her sword and strike at the air around her was overwhelming. The only thing holding her back was the concern that she might harm Maren.

"Answer me!" she shouted. "Please!"

Suddenly, the wind calmed and the growling stopped. The fire re-kindled, and all was still. Faymia looked around the camp to discover that she was all alone. Maren's blanket was gone from the ground and there was no sign of her.

A great sense of sorrow filled Faymia's heart and invisible weights sat upon her shoulders, so she sat on the ground and wept. It must have been for a very long time because she felt exhausted from sobbing. She lay down and let fatigue take her as she closed her eyes. As she did, the hushed voice inside of her was able to be heard, and she felt a small amount of encouragement in the awareness that it was only a dream.

>>>

Faymia awoke the next morning feeling rested but sore. Her neck ached, and she had to bend and extend her leg several times to work out the stiffness before she could swing it over the side of the bed. To her surprise, her cheek was wet from tears, and her heart was still heavy from her dream.

Sitting up, she watched Maren sleeping nearby in a large stuffed chair. A tentative sense of relief filled her heart as she observed the girl's deep, unconscious breaths.

The room was dimly lit by a single lantern perched on a chest of drawers near the door. It was hard to tell whether it was actually morning or still night, since there were no windows to let in the outside light.

The room was furnished with fine furniture, and ornate rugs were laid across the stone floor. However, it still had a cave-like feel to it, as the walls were carved from the same black rock that the entire eastern cliff was formed from. The woman found it curious to see dark wood wainscoting running from the floor to midway up the walls. She felt it was akin to putting a dress on a beast of burden or hanging a chandelier in a barn.

Slipping on her boots, she quietly walked to the door and opened it most of the way. Looking out, she tried to gauge the best direction to walk that would lead her toward the cave's opening. When she was brought to the dwelling, her eyes were covered and it was very late at night. And when she was finally shown to her room, there were so many twists and turns through strange, torchlit hallways that she wasn't even sure she could find her way back to the chief's chamber.

The woman leaned out into the hall. Seeing the same smooth, black rock forming the walls, floors, and ceilings, she wondered how long it must have taken to create the homes of the Ruhbrem. Through the cool, clammy air she could smell coffee brewing and slowly began to follow the scent down a hall that gradually sloped downward and made a hard turn to the right. It ran the opposite direction from where she had imagined the cave's opening to be.

As she continued on, the hallway began to broaden and open up to other passages. She was curious to know where they led but decided to follow the scent of what she hoped to be breakfast.

Suddenly, there was a scuffling of feet behind her and she spun around. Maren stood there expressionless with her hand on her ear.

Faymia clutched the front of her tunic and calmed herself. The sudden appearance of another person in the dark, deserted halls almost had her drawing her sword. "Maren," she gasped. "I wasn't going to be gone long. I thought you were asleep."

"The smell of coffee woke me up," the girl explained. She then smelled the air and added, "And eggs, and bread, and"—sniffing the air one more time—"and jam."

Impressed, the woman raised her eyebrows, closed her eye, and inhaled deeply through her nose. "Well, you're the one with the magnificent sniffer, aren't you. I only smell the coffee."

"The rest is there," Maren said plainly and began to make her way past Faymia, turning down one of the passages.

Faymia followed closely behind until several voices could be heard in lively chatter amidst the sounds of clanging eating utensils and shifting chairs. When they entered the room, she realized they were back in Thuaid's chamber. Only this time, it looked different. Candles adorned every part of the room, washing it in dancing, orange-yellow light. The center of the table was stuffed with platters of eggs, fresh bread, bowls of butter, and strawberry jam. Maren didn't wait for an invitation. She skipped over to an open chair and sat down. There was a clean plate sitting on the table in front of her, and she began helping herself to heaping mounds of food.

"There she is!" one of the woman servants announced. "How are ye, girl?" she asked Maren.

"Fine," she said, already spreading a generous helping of jam on a thick slice of bread.

Then, above the clamor, Thuaid's voice rang out, "Good morning, everyone!"

Faymia could see the man rising from the chair nearest the front of the room. On either side of him were the aides that questioned her the night before. There were also a handful of others that gave her the impression they were of some importance. "Good morning," she returned along with everyone else.

Looking at Faymia, the man invited, "Please, have a seat," and he gestured toward an empty place next to where Maren was filling her stomach.

"Thank you," the woman replied, and she settled next to her friend. It felt awkward to be joining the group for a meal. It felt much like attending a family gathering of strangers, and the conversation was of things of which she had no knowledge.

As she prepared a plate for herself, she felt a tap on her right shoulder. Turning around, she saw a familiar man crouch next to her. It was one of the chief's assistants from the night before. "Hello, my name is Argach," the man introduced himself.

Faymia didn't like speaking to him. After the prior night's events, she had hoped to never see either of the men again. Her shoulders tightened, and she found it difficult to maintain eye contact with him. "Hello," she replied.

Argach's features were much softer than before. He glanced at the floor, then back toward the woman. "I'm very sorry for the way I treated you last night," he said. "It was...unbecoming."

The woman was taken aback. An apology was the last thing she had expected from the man. For the first time she noticed that he had ginger hair and blue eyes. He had a lean build and his hands were strong and worn, like the chief's. "What's done is done," she muttered.

With a half-smile the man replied, "No, I shouldn't have been so rough. It's just that I thought you were one of them. A lowgrounder. That probably sounds terrible."

Still slightly thrown by the man's penitence, Faymia answered, "Maybe a little. But I understand. I've been there myself." She then forced a sympathetic smile and hoped it reinforced her words of forgiveness.

"Thank you for your understanding," Argach said.

Still thinking about the night before, Faymia gestured across the table to the other man who had interrogated her. He was loud, and brass, and seemed to fully enjoy the attention he was currently getting from the other people around the table. "What about him?" Faymia asked. "He was much more harsh with me than you were."

"Oh, that's Gadoar," he said. "He's our village scout.

He keeps an eye on the lowgrounders for us and reports back to the chief."

"Is he always so..." the woman began.

"Boisterous?" Argach said, finishing her sentence with a slight grimace.

"I was going to say passionate," Faymia stated. "Or maybe it was obnoxious, or braggadocios." She held back a giggle and bit her tongue, wanting to add many other adjectives to the man's description.

The man chuckled. "He's an acquired taste, but he means well. And he does a great job at keeping everyone informed."

"I'm sure he does," she replied with a hint of suspicion in her eye.

Just then, Thuaid stood up from the table and walked over to join the conversation. As he did, the woman to the right of Faymia offered her seat to the man. He casually accepted the gesture and sat down. "How did you sleep?" he asked with a smile.

Faymia wasn't quite sure how to answer the question. She didn't know how late it was when she was shown to her room, and she still hadn't seen the sun at all yet this morning. For all she knew, she had only slept for an hour before wandering down the hall. "Fine," she answered, stretching the word out to two syllables so it almost sounded like a question.

"Ah, grand," the chief grinned. "And how about the little Maren?"

The young girl had just stuffed the oversized last remaining bite of her bread into her mouth. Barely able to annunciate, she muffled out, "Good!" then walked to the other side of the table to join the others in giving their attention to Gadoar.

"Is she yours?" Thuaid asked. An awkward expression crawled over his face that revealed he wasn't confident in the appropriateness of his question.

"In a manner," she said. "She's under my care."

"I see." He then raised an eyebrow as he rubbed his chin. Haltingly, he asked, "Is she...normal?"

Faymia watched Maren interact with the scout and the others around her. They were all very amused by her, but she knew well what the chief was getting at. A sense of indignation crept over her and kept her from answering directly. Instead, she asked, "What do you mean by normal?"

Thuaid shifted in his seat. His face went blank and he stammered, "Well, you know, behaves well, communicates clearly, keeps up appearances, gets along with others. Things like that."

The woman forced a smile and replied, "By that definition, we are all abnormal at times."

"I'm sorry," the man spluttered. "I didn't mean to offend." Then, widening his eyes and leaning forward, he said, "Look, I would love to answer any questions you have about the Ohdium. You said your mother was from here. I'm sure you have lots of questions."

Faymia leaned back in her chair a bit, now satisfied from breakfast and the uncomfortable feeling she apparently gave the chief. There was so much she would like to know about this place, but what pressed her the most was the incredible divide between its people. "I think I'd like to know how you became separated into two tribes," she said.

Thuaid continued to smile but his back straightened and his shoulders broadened as he seemed to be searching his memories for the answer. "Well, we have always had more than one chief leading the people of the Ohdium. As many as five or six at one point. We lived as one people, and the leaders served the people to the best of our ability." As he spoke, his eyes drifted toward the ceiling as if he were looking back in time toward better days.

Faymia thought about what the man was saying and compared it to what she had experienced the night before. "That sounds lovely," she said. "But how did you get from there to the state of affairs now?"

"I suppose it began when those living below grew discontented with living in the woods and fields. They called us the Aougur Folk, the high and mighty wastrels, and began to disparage us in tribal meetings. As I mentioned last night, they tried usurping our dwellings, and they raised taxes on farming land that we hired from them. We were forced to farm atop the cliffs instead." As the chief spoke, his face took on a reddish hue and his voice became louder and more passionate. "Eventually, the many tribes merged into only two, each with the hopes of over-coming the other with their combined resources," he added.

The woman listened and tried to process what was being said. However, she couldn't help but feel that much of the story was missing. She was going to ask more questions, but felt it would only cause the man to froth at the mouth as he complained about the lowground Taalbrem people. "Well, it is unfortunate that such a beautiful place is filled with so much discord," was all she could say.

"Indeed," Thuaid muttered as he caught his breath.

Faymia smiled politely and thought about returning to the Neodrec to gather her horse and belongings. But, glancing across the room for Maren, she did not see her. "Where did my companion go?" she asked no one in particular.

One of the women gathering dishes from the table chirped, "Oh, she ran after Gadoar. I think she's taken a shining to him!"

Faymia's stomach turned. It had already been a dangerous experience for them both, and she had hoped to keep the girl in her sights. Especially after the dream she had during the night.

"It's all right," Thuaid tried to assure. "Gadoar is trustworthy, and wouldn't let any harm come to her."

The woman was not comforted by the man's words one bit. Her neck stiffened and her heart began to race as she swiftly made her way out the door.

# CHAPTER FIVE
## BLESSED ONE

Maren followed Gadoar along a broad wooden walkway that wove its way from side to side and up and down along the face of the eastern cliff. It looked much different than the old, abandoned dwellings they discovered the day before. Besides being well kept, they were much higher up. And the view west over the neutral zone and rolling, wooded hills beyond was breathtaking. The walkway was wide and sturdy enough for foot pedestrians to go to and fro without getting in each other's way. As she passed by homes and shops carved out of the dense, black stone, she would occasionally reach out to touch the ornate carvings along their exterior.

The scout walked briskly through the vertical village and didn't seem to notice that the young girl was following him. He wore expensive-looking clothes, and his dark, handsome features lit up when people would stop to ask if he had any news of the tensions between the Ruhbrem and Taalbrem. "Ah, those scoundrels tried attacking us last night," he said to a woman sweeping the walkway in front of her dwelling.

"Really?" she gasped, nearly dropping her broom.

"They are completely without integrity," he replied. "Absolute savages."

They walked until the boarded path stopped at a large split in the rock face. Then, two flights of stairs took them down toward a lower walkway. Gadoar was greeted by yet another admirer and he smiled widely as he told them how the chief was committed to stomping out the evil of the lowgrounder plague, and that better days will come when the Ruhbrem control the entire Rift. This went on for quite a while, as the man seemed committed to stopping each time a villager asked him about the ongoing conflict.

Finally reaching the lowest tier of the walkway, Gadoar was asked by a blacksmith if he was on his way to scout the Taalbrem. "Indeed I am," he answered enthusiastically. "The enemy never sleeps, so I must remain ever vigilant."

"Good on you," the blacksmith cheered. "Thank you for all you do!"

"It's my pleasure," the scout replied with a wink.

When he reached the end of the lowest tier, it turned sharply in the opposite direction, becoming a gradually descending ramp the length of the walkway above.

Maren was no longer entertained by the man. Nor did she wish to catch up with him. She was now intensely interested in how he gathered his information about the lowgrounders, and assumed that following him undetected would be the best way to find out.

As she followed him across the Neodrec, she stayed a good distance behind and wove around patches of tall shrubbery, large stones, and trees. It was difficult because the flat ground was mostly barren until it reached the area where it began to slope upward into Taalbrem territory.

She followed him into an area where pine trees grew together, shading lifeless ground covered in brown needles and dead pine cones. Moving just past the small forest, it opened up to a field that rolled on into the distance before reaching another wooded area.

To Maren's surprise, another man was waiting in the field for the scout just beyond the tree line. He glared at Gadoar and scoffed, "It's about time!"

"Can I help it if I'm popular?" Gadoar retorted.

Maren crouched quietly within the cover of the pines. Massaging her ear and listening intently, she tried to make sense of what the men were saying. Eventually, they walked further afield until she could no longer see or hear them. Not wanting to risk being discovered, she turned around to make her way across the wooded area and back up to the chief's dwelling.

As she spun around, she was snatched up by two muscular arms that lifted her off the ground and a voice growled, "What are you doing here, highground brat?!"

>>>———•———

"Put me down!" Maren shouted.

She flailed and kicked to try to break herself free from the muscular, bare arms that held onto her, but it was like fighting against a tree.

"Shut up!" her captor yelled back. "You're a spy and I'm taking you for questioning!"

Maren thought about biting the arms that held her tightly, but they were covered in sweat, and questioning seemed much more bearable than a mouthful of perspiration. She looked around and saw that they were traveling north on a well-worn trail between the woods to the east and the fields to the west. She knew that, if she escaped, she could dart into the woods and eventually make her way into the neutral zone. She broadened her shoulders, kicked furiously, and tried to wiggle her way to the ground.

Suddenly, the arms that held her constricted until she could no longer breathe. "You're hurting me!" she gasped.

"Try that again, and I'll break your back!" the person yelled.

Maren relaxed. As she did, she found that the pressure on her body relieved and she was able to breathe again.

"You are wise to cooperate," her captor threatened. "Don't make this any more difficult than it needs to be."

As her capturer spoke, Maren realized something about the voice. Unable to keep the thought to herself, she blurted out, "Hey, you're a woman!"

"You're just now noticing that?" the voice behind the muscular arms asked. She then released a low growl and quickened her pace toward the lowground village.

"How did you get such big arms?" the girl asked.

"I said to shut up!" the sturdy woman shouted, leaning her head slightly forward so that her command was aimed directly at Maren's right ear.

Maren winced. She didn't like sudden, loud noises and her head jerked back, hitting the woman's upper lip.

"Ouch!" the woman cried. "I ought to kill you for that!"

"I'm sorry!" Maren exclaimed. "I didn't mean to!" She then braced herself for whatever punishment the woman was going to dole out.

"Well, don't do that again. The next time, I'll do it back!" she threatened.

Maren felt like she should reply, but didn't want to stoke her captor's anger any further. "Yes, ma'am," she muttered.

Up ahead, the young girl could see the path sloping upward. As it did, it opened up and she could see a tall tree and the rooftops of several structures. Once they reached the top of the footpath, the woman began to move even faster. Doing so caused Maren to jostle up and down in her arms, making it difficult to take in their surroundings.

"There's the chief's dwelling," the muscular woman announced, and soon they were inside one of the village's buildings.

***

Maren found herself in a large hall similar to Thuaid's. Many of the same beautiful symbols adorned the legs of the table and the beams that ran from the floor to the high ceiling. She was surprised at how similar the room was to the one in the cliffs, noting that the biggest difference was the inclusion of windows behind the chief's chair. They opened up to gray skies and rolling wheat fields that swayed as a breeze gently pushed them to and fro.

"Girl!" the man on the wooden throne barked. "What were you doing in the border woods?"

Maren was still shaken by the rough treatment she

received. She was swept off her feet by the burly, bare-armed woman who now stood next to her with her hand on the girl's shoulder.

Maren massaged her ear and glanced at the ceiling. She was beginning to sweat, and a smothering anxiety threatened to keep her mouth locked shut. "Um, watching," she answered reluctantly.

The chief squinted his blue eyes and cocked his head. His skin was rough and tan, and he wore his blond-and-silver hair back in a braid. If not for his white beard, he would have looked much younger than he currently did. "What were you watching?" he asked.

Fearing that she would be tried and hung as a spy, she answered, "A lark."

The man's eyes seemed to look deeper into the girl, almost as if he recognized her but couldn't remember her name. "And why did you leave the highground side of the Rift?" he asked.

Maren continued rubbing her ear. There was a tremor in her voice. "I don't live there," she said.

The burly woman squeezed her shoulder and shook it. "Well, you don't live HERE!" she shouted.

The girl startled and almost fell to the floor. "No, I don't," she attempted to answer through quivering lips.

"Easy, Soeth!" the chief shouted. "Take your hand off of her and step away."

Maren felt relieved to have the woman's knotty paw off of her. Her mouth was dry, and she attempted to swallow as she answered again, "I don't live here either."

Once again, the white-bearded man looked deeply at Maren. Then, as if an invisible messenger had whispered something into his ear, his face relaxed and his voice softened. "Girl, come closer."

She moved a few baby steps closer to the man, still attempting to comfort herself with her hand on her ear. "Yes, sir."

"What is your name?" he asked.

"Maren," she answered plainly. She then looked back at the rough woman who captured her. She was now leaning against the long wall that ran from the entrance of the room to the tall windows.

"It's all right," the chief assured. "She won't bother you. That's Soeth, my chief security officer. She's a fierce protector, and you can't be too careful these days. My name is Le'as." He then paused and took a deep breath. "Do you mind if I ask you," he began. Then, as if searching for the right words, he fumbled, "Do you have... I mean... are you... with the graymind?"

Maren was familiar with the term. She had heard her parents use it, and remembered Dulnear saying that she had it when they first met. She simply nodded her head yes in reply.

"Never mind," the man assured. "In our village, people with the graymind are highly esteemed. We treasure your uniqueness, and you have a special place among us."

Maren could barely believe what she was hearing. The room felt as if it were swaying back and forth. She glanced back at Soeth. Though the chief and his attendants were now smiling at the girl, the muscular security officer stood stony-faced with arms folded.

"How do you feel about that?" Le'as asked with an uncomfortably enthusiastic grin.

"Fine," the girl answered, though she really didn't know how she was feeling.

"I apologize for the way you were brought here. There were reports of a highground attack last night, and we are all on edge here," the man explained. "I would very much like to show you around our hamlet. Would you like that?"

"Yes," Maren responded, though she was still trying to understand what had happened since being grabbed and brought to the chief's chamber.

Just then, an out-of-breath young messenger ran into the room and went straight to Le'as. "Pardon me," he interrupted. "There are stirrings of a large-scale attack from the Ruhbrem!"

The chief sat up and looked gravely at the man. As they exchanged words, Maren observed the messenger closely. Suddenly, she recognized him as the one that Gadoar had met when he crossed into the lowground territory.

When they finished talking, Le'as called Soeth over. After speaking quietly to her, he sent her off with the young man. "I'm sorry," he said. "That was my scout, Breag. It looks like last night's skirmish was only the beginning. The Ruhbrem have something even greater planned."

Maren resumed massaging her ear. She wondered if the attack that she and Faymia endured the night before was related to what the chief was talking about. However, she did not bring it up for fear that she would have to deal with Soeth once more. She simply shrugged and forced a smile.

"I'll be joining them shortly," he continued. "But first, I'm going to show you around, just as I promised. It will be a brief tour, but there's always time for our blessed ones."

Exiting the chief's house, Maren realized that the windows at the rear of his chamber had been facing west. The village was built along a street that began where the path she arrived on ended, and turned back into a path once there were no more structures that lined it. The houses and shops that made up the tiny town mostly faced east toward a narrow field that rolled downward into a strip of forest that bordered the Neodrec.

A short distance east from the entrance of the house was an odd stone carving that stood five times as tall as a man. To Maren, it looked like a tree made of three large ropes that twisted together to form the trunk and branches. All along the stone rope strands were carved symbols, much like the ones she had seen all over the Ohdium, but they were even more intricate and beautiful to her. Surrounding the tree was a stone table that formed a circle around its trunk. Engraved across the table was the word "Soshayne."

"What is that?" she asked.

"That is the Reonem," Le'as said. A hint of sadness appeared on his face as they walked closer to it. "It was our reasoning table when we were united as one people. We used to gather for hours celebrating the good things happening for each other, working out our differences, and making the Rift a better place for our families." Suddenly, his countenance changed and he added, "But that was before those greedy Ruhbrem decided they were too good for us lowground folk."

"They did?" the girl asked, scratching the top of her head.

"Indeed," the chief responded. "In fact, they won't even let blessed ones like yourself live among them."

Upon hearing that, Maren was taken aback. She pushed her forehead forward and massaged her ear. "Well, where do they live then?" she asked.

"I don't know," the man said. "But they are not allowed to live in the highground village."

As those words sank in, the girl looked up at the strange tree statue and the symbols adorning it. Feeling uncomfortable, she changed the subject. "Can I see the rest of the village?" she asked.

"Of course," the man chirped, and they began to walk south along the shops and homes that lay neatly along the road that ran in front of the buildings. As they did, they stopped in front of a feed shop. The owner, an unreasonably sweaty-looking man in a green apron, was sitting on a wooden chair in front of the shop, sipping water. "Hiya, Raith!" Le'as greeted with a smile.

"Hiya, Chief," the man replied, standing up to shake the chief's hand.

"Say, where's William today?" Le'as asked.

"Oh, he's in the back watering the animals," the shopkeeper said as he sat back down and took a sip from his tin cup.

"Well, I'm giving my friend Maren here a tour of the village," the chief explained. "I'd like to introduce her to your boy when we come back this way. Is that all right with you?"

"I'm sure he'd be happy with that," the man said. "And it's very nice to meet you, young lady."

Maren smiled and nodded her head. She muttered, "Same," and the two of them continued walking south.

The town seemed to have been built beginning with the chief's house (being the oldest of its structures) and spread outward. Its chronology could be seen in its architecture, with each building built north or south of its center looking newer than the last. The girl noticed that the buildings that were built most recently didn't look as solidly built as the others. She also noticed that the emblems that adorned most of the other structures in the Rift were missing. Walking past one of the last houses on the southern edge, she reached out to touch the door and asked, "Where are the pictures for this one?"

"Oh, you mean the taek," Le'as said. "I'm afraid those symbols are from times long gone."

"Why are they gone?" she queried.

The chief looked eastward toward the sloping fields and the forest beyond. He then looked down at the girl with a wistful smile and answered, "Before we were two groups, we combined our skills and resources to create many things, like the reasoning table and the taek. These homes were built after the Great Divide, and that's why there are no symbols on them."

Maren loved the beauty of the taek. She couldn't fathom why people would choose to live in a way that diminished the splendor of what could be accomplished together. "Why don't you just team up again?" the girl asked as they turned around and began walking north toward the center of the village.

Le'as laughed. "I wish it were that easy, my friend. Unfortunately, the highgrounders cannot be trusted or reasoned with. My scout reports to me about all of the vile things those people are doing, every day."

Maren thought about her experience with the Ruhbrem. The servants were kind to her, and Thuaid seemed like a decent man, in her estimation. Optimistically, she hummed, "Maybe someday."

"Maybe," the man repeated. As they walked closer to the feed shop, he pointed and said, "Oh look, there's William. Let me introduce you to him."

The girl wasn't expecting to see what she did. Moving closer, she saw a boy about her own age. He was seated on a mat on the ground. Upon further examination, she realized that both of his legs were missing. She wasn't expecting such a sight. Swallowing, she croaked, "All right."

"Hello there, William," Le'as called out. "How are you this afternoon?"

"Hi, Le'as," the boy replied with a smile. He wore a coif on his head that seemed to want to crawl forward toward his eyes. He balanced his body with his right hand and waved a leather-gloved left hand at the chief.

Le'as knelt down to be eye to eye with William. Smiling, he gestured toward Maren and beamed, "This is Maren. I thought the two of you could be great pals."

Maren massaged her ear and studied the boy. She was impressed by how muscular his body was, and wondered if she could get a pair of gloves like his. "Hello," she said plainly.

"Hello," the boy grinned back, wiggling the fingers on his left hand.

"See, we have many blessed ones like you and William

here," the chief began. "They are among the most prized members of our community."

Maren gasped and took a step back. "I'm not like him," she exclaimed. "He doesn't have any legs!"

Le'as turned red. Lowering his voice, he explained, "I don't mean that you're the same. I just mean that you're both special."

The girl didn't understand what he was getting at. "But how could he be special if he doesn't even have legs?" she asked.

The chief winced and looked at William, who was now hanging his head. "He's special BECAUSE he doesn't have legs," he said.

Maren surveyed the boy again, hoping that if she spoke louder and clearer, the man would understand her better. "That's not special. Special is having great skill, or speed, or strength. There is nothing special about not having legs."

Poor William was now weeping. He allowed his hat to completely cover his eyes as he tried to keep his face from being seen by the girl.

"Yes, but he IS very special," the man tried explaining again. Just then, Soeth sprinted up to the feed shop, interrupting the awkward conversation.

"Le'as, you must come with me now," she announced. "I have important news of the Ruhbrem's plans, and we need to assemble the defense council immediately."

The chief stood to his feet. "I'm sorry," he said, pushing his mouth to one side of his face. "Why don't the two of you, er, get to know each other." He then rushed off with his chief security officer.

Maren stood there alone with William. "I like your gloves," she monotoned.

He reached up and pushed his hat back, wiping the tears from his eyes. "Thanks," he replied, still not looking at her.

"Well, I have to get back to my friend, Faymia," she explained, and took a tiny step backward.

"Sure," William said as he shifted himself away from her and began to head back into his father's shop.

Maren stood there for a moment and watched the boy leave. Something inside of her said that she should have responded differently to the situation, but she didn't know how. "Bye," she murmured quietly toward him. She then headed east down the field toward the border woods, hoping to find Faymia on the other side of the Rift.

CHAPTER SIX

# BEAUTY AND POWER

"Excuse me, have you seen a little girl?" Faymia asked.

It was the fifth person she'd questioned as she navigated her way down the wooden path that ran back and forth along the black cliff that contained the Ruhbrem village. So far, no one had claimed to have laid eyes on Maren since she followed Gadoar out of the chief's chamber. The woman was growing more concerned with each passing moment, and her pace quickened as she moved on to the next shop. There were children browsing its aisles, and she hoped to find Maren among them.

Having no luck at that place, she went to the next, and the next, only to experience increasing disappointment with each conversation. About halfway down the walkway, she came across a shop selling only books. *Surely they've seen her here*, she thought to herself.

The store was much larger on the inside than Faymia expected it to be. A spark of hope arose in her. Believing that the girl could be tucked away reading in some corner of the shop, she forced herself to move slowly and carefully, searching the rows of reading material. As she moved systematically past each shelf, she became even more anxious until she had covered the entire business without seeing Maren, and the spark of hope faded away.

Before leaving, she approached the proprietor. He was a round, middle-aged man who wore ill-fitting clothing and looked to be losing his unwashed hair. He sat behind the counter with his face in an enormous tome, and made no indication that he even noticed someone was standing before him.

"Excuse me," Faymia said politely, but there was no response. Again, she tried to gain the man's attention. "Ahem," she cleared her throat. "Pardon me."

When the man continued to ignore her, she could feel whatever calm she was clinging to quickly fade and she slammed her hand down upon the counter. "Hey!" she barked. "You are being terribly rude!"

The man looked up from the book with an expression that told Faymia that she was actually the rude one, and that she had better get on with her business quickly.

"I'm looking for a little girl," she began. "She has dark hair, and is wearing a blue apron with flowers embroidered on it. Have you seen her?"

"Probably not," the man said plainly as his eyes seemed to be pulled back to the book by an invisible force.

"What do you mean by probably?" Faymia asked. "Do you mean that children have been here, but you're not sure if one of them was the one I'm looking for?"

"I mean that no child has been here," the man snapped. "And if one was, they would have been thrown out for disturbing me." He then tilted his balding head forward and added, "And if you continue to be a nuisance, you will be thrown out too."

The woman's nostrils flared and she balled her hand into a fist. "It's a miracle you're still in business," she chided, and spun around to leave.

Darting out of the store and down the path, Faymia's imagination began to go to dark places and her mind conjured images of a badly injured Maren. Just before she reached the end of the tier she was jogging along, a voice called out, "Are you looking for a little girl?"

Faymia stopped and saw an old woman sitting on a stool in front of a small dwelling. She looked much poorer than the other inhabitants she had met in the Rift, and she seemed to be staring out into the chasm beyond the walkway. "What was that?" she asked, approaching the woman.

"I asked if you were looking for a little girl," the old woman said. She was sitting up as straight as a board. Yet, from the waist up, she was rocking herself forward and backward in a peculiar fashion.

Faymia drew even closer. Her heart leapt at the idea that someone might know the whereabouts of Maren. "Yes, I am," she exclaimed. She held her hand in the air to show an estimation of the girl's height. "She is about this tall, has dark hair, and is wearing a blue apron. Have you seen her?"

The woman didn't turn her head to look at Faymia's hand. Instead, she chuckled, "I haven't seen anything in years."

It finally dawned on Faymia that the woman was blind. Suddenly, the lines in her face seemed deeper, and the milky haze over her eyes more evident. Feeling a bit embarrassed, she asked, "How did you know I was looking for someone?"

The woman pointed a swollen, bent finger toward the side of her head. "These ears of mine work wonderfully," she said. "I've heard you ask at least eight people about her."

Faymia was amused, but was far too anxious to spend any more time with her. She had lost Maren once before and couldn't bear the thought of losing her again. "I'm sorry," she began. "I would love to stay and visit, but I really must find her."

"I understand," the blind woman said. "May I ask you a question?"

Trying not to let her voice betray her impatience, Faymia replied, "Go ahead."

"Was she with Gadoar the scout this morning?" the old woman asked.

"Why, yes. She followed him out of the chief's chamber after breakfast."

The blind woman's rocking motion picked up speed and took on an excited quality. She grinned broadly and exclaimed, "Every morning that rascal parades on down to the Neodrec, shaking hands and telling stories like he's campaigning to be the chief. He laps up the attention like it is sweet custard."

"But, what about my friend?" Faymia asked.

"Oh, yes," the blind woman said, pulling herself back to the reason they were talking. She then exhaled, and it was as if all the excitement she previously displayed flowed out of her body and ran down the walkway.

Faymia noticed the mysterious shift in the woman's

demeanor, and the village seemed strangely quiet for a moment. "Are you all right?" she asked.

"Of course," the elder said calmly. "I'll get to your friend in a moment. Before I do, can I ask you for something?"

"Anything," she replied. "I just really need to find her."

"Then please, bring your face here so I can touch it."

Faymia felt as if the entire cliffside was swaying on a gigantic boat. She was uncomfortable with the woman's request but was willing to do anything to find Maren again. She knelt closely on both knees and announced, "I'm directly in front of you."

The old woman reached out and began to examine her face with her hands. She gently removed the leather covering over her left eye and caressed the scar that the northerner Searfain left behind.

To Faymia's surprise, the woman's hands were soft and clean, and smelled faintly of lavender. Something about her touch set her at ease and she relaxed as her fingertips moved over every part of her face with patience and grace.

"Hmmmm," the old woman murmured. She then took a deep breath and smiled.

"What is it?" Faymia asked. "Is it my scar? I lost the use of my eye in—"

Interrupting, the woman continued. "No, dear. It's not the scar. It's the overwhelming power." A tear escaped her eye and ran down her cheek. "And such beauty."

Faymia was taken aback by her remark. She wanted to pull her face away, but remained. As she spoke, a tear ran down her own cheek and she muttered, "I don't understand."

"Of course, but one day, you will," the blind woman assured. "So many have power but no beauty in them. And many more have beauty but no true power. I feel both in you."

Faymia felt something rise up inside of her. It was an urge to both laugh and cry at the same time. A sense of lightness and responsibility came together within her, and many of the vague shadows of insecurity and deficiency were replaced with confident calm. "Thank you," she sniffled. She knelt for seconds that felt like hours until the image of Maren filled her mind again. Moving back slightly, she took the old woman's hands into her own and asked, "But what about my friend?"

"Yes, about Maren," the blind woman began. "I heard her dainty little footsteps following Gadoar all the way down to the neutral territory, and beyond. I love the way she whispers to herself."

Faymia quickly slid her eye patch back on and stood up. "Thank you! A million times thank you!" she exclaimed.

The old, blind woman smiled from ear to ear, and she resumed her peculiar rocking. "It's my pleasure, sweetheart," she said. "Thank you for letting me see you."

Faymia bent down and threw her arms around the woman's shoulders. As she did, the lavender scent filled her nostrils and, for a moment, she didn't want to let go. "I hope to talk with you again," she said, and stood to leave.

The old woman smiled, then tilted her head to one side as if straining to hear something far away. The corner of her mouth turned upward and she said quietly, "The most blessed songs have many harmonies, wouldn't you agree?"

Faymia froze with bewilderment at the unexpectedly

random statement. She thought perhaps the woman was senile, but something about her told her otherwise. Desperately wanting to find Maren, she answered, "They certainly do. Again, thank you." And she darted down the walkway and across the Neodrec.

>>>———·———

As Faymia entered the woods beyond the neutral zone, the words of the old woman echoed in her mind. She wanted to rush back and speak to her more, but she was driven to find Maren. She was able to detect a few of the footprints the girl had left behind, but lost them in the clearing blanketed in pine needles.

She stopped, breathed in the forest air, and listened, hoping that the direction she should take would make itself known to her. To her discouragement, she felt nothing.

Unexpectedly, the sound of someone stepping on dead twigs came from the other side of the clearing. She peered and saw Gadoar, who looked just as surprised to see her as she was to see him. "Gadoar!" she shouted. "Am I glad to see you!"

"You are?" he muttered. He then looked around and asked, "What are you doing here?"

"I'm looking for Maren," she explained. "She followed you out of Thuaid's chamber this morning."

The scout squinted and scratched his head. "She did? Well, I doubt she came this far. There's nothing for a child to see here."

"A woman in the village said she followed you across the

Neodrec," Faymia continued. "Are you sure you didn't see her?"

Gadoar crossed his arms and planted his feet. His face turned a shade of pink as he swallowed. "What woman?" he asked.

"The blind woman in front of the dwelling just beyond the bookstore," she said.

The scout glared at her condescendingly. "No one lives there, and there are no blind women among the Ruhbrem," he scowled.

"No blind women?" Faymia gasped. "Well, I'm sure I didn't imagine her."

"Perhaps you were deceived, or mistaken," Gadoar grunted. "The blind, the crippled, even those whose minds are different, all live atop the cliffs in the Blessed Lands." He then continued. "They are held in very high esteem, and are treated with utmost care there."

"So you have a separate village for them?" Faymia asked.

"That is correct. It is the finest land on the eastern side. Your friend Maren would be welcome there. As would you, considering the permanent injury to your eye."

Faymia didn't like having attention brought to her eye, and had never considered it to be an injury requiring assistance for daily living. She considered his words an insult, but held back from responding to it. Not wanting to argue the realities of blind women among the Ruhbrem cliff dwellers, she simply said, "Well, I'm going to poke around the woods a bit to see if I can find her."

Gadoar's lip twitched and his eyes looked beyond Faymia. "You probably shouldn't do that. It isn't safe," he admonished.

"I'm sure I'll be fine," she assured. "I really need to find her before the day gets late."

"Listen, these lowground leches care not that you are a woman. They'll attack and kill you without remorse," the scout warned.

Something in Faymia's mind convinced her that the man was trying to stir fear where there was no need for it. In a polite yet firm tone she answered, "I'm not leaving here without Maren. I'll take my chances."

Gritting his teeth, the scout hissed, "As you wish, but you were warned."

To Faymia's surprise, Gadoar turned around and went back toward the lowground side of the ravine. There was much about the man she didn't like, and she suspected there was a side to him that he was keeping hidden.

***

As the afternoon light started to wane, Son could feel the perspiration on his neck begin to chill so he threw on his gray coat and buttoned it to the top as he sat in his usual place near the fire. His body felt tired, but his mind stayed busy as it repeatedly rehearsed all that he had learned that day. In his thoughts he was swift, strong, and a match for any attacker.

"Your hard work is paying off," Dulnear beamed as he sat across the fire from him. "You would give any northern boy a run for his money. Including myself at your age."

"Thanks!" Son smiled. "I was hoping we could work more with the dagger after we rest."

"If that is what you wish," his mentor said. He then

withdrew one from beneath his coat and began reviewing the various components that made the weapon so deadly.

As he spoke, Son noticed the silhouette of a large figure moving in the trees that surrounded the mountain shelf. It startled him, and he reached for his sword as he sprang to his feet.

Dulnear spun around and flung the knife with surprising speed and accuracy. There was a whoosh and a clang as the figure blocked the dagger with his sword and it fell harmlessly to the ground.

Son rushed toward the trees. Something in him compelled him to attack, and he didn't hear his friend call out to wait.

Stepping out from the woods a large, blond-haired, blue-eyed, fur-clad man met the boy with an enormous boot to the chest, sending him backward through the air. Son grasped at his chest, frantically trying to regain his breath as he struggled to his feet. As he did, he noticed Dulnear running past him, toward the man. There was a brief clashing of swords that ended as abruptly as it began.

"Dulnear, it is me!" the figure shouted.

"Why did you kick the boy?" Dulnear asked, still holding his sword at the ready.

Son moved to where he could see the unwelcome visitor more clearly, but kept a safe distance so he wouldn't become collateral damage in a scuffle between two northerners.

"*He* attacked *me*," the other man said.

"You have been lurking around our camp for days," Dulnear pointed out. "What did you expect?"

"I was waiting for a moment when I would not alert you," he explained.

"You know that is impossible," Dulnear stated. He then released the air from his lungs and added, "You should have thrown a rock with a note on it into the camp."

"A rock with a note?" the man asked. "Are you serious?"

"Maybe," Dulnear mumbled. "At least it would have been better than creeping about."

"Next time," the man promised with a slight grin. His shoulders relaxed and he put away his weapon.

"Son, this is Brunnlyn," Dulnear introduced, backing away from the man and sheathing his sword.

A bit confused by the interaction that had just taken place, the boy followed his friend's example. "My pleasure," he said, nodding his head slightly.

"This immense buck had a part in having my hand removed," Dulnear croaked as he returned to the fire.

Brunnlyn returned Son's nod, and the three of them found a place to sit. After a moment of awkward silence, the man began, "I am very sorry for the intrusion, and I definitely did not mean to alarm anyone."

"We are here training," Dulnear explained. "Son is my pupil, and friend." He then paused for a moment and scratched his neck. "I am very surprised to see you alive," he admitted. "After killing Thorndel, I thought you would be dead for sure."

"Worse," the man said. He then held up his right arm, revealing that his hand had been cleanly removed. All that remained was a pink, burn-scarred stump. "The shame was unbearable. For a time, I considered ending my own life."

Dulnear looked down at the end of his own right arm.

He closed his eyes for a moment and admitted, "I know that feeling. I will never understand why you would do that for me."

"I did not do it for you," Brunnlyn said. "It was for me."

"What do you mean?" Dulnear asked as his eyes grew wide.

"I saw that you had escaped," the man said. "You found a way to free yourself from the endless violence of Tuas-Arum, and I was ready to do the same, even if it meant being considered as walking dead by my kinsmen."

Dulnear sat frozen with an expression of disbelief. Finally, he muttered, "I do not know what to say."

"There is no need to say anything," Brunnlyn stated. "I should be thanking you. You were willing to die to make restitution with Shenndel. You showed me that the path of peace, though infinitely more difficult to stay on, is better than forever proving your power over others. I have found a better way to exist because of your example."

Son looked back and forth between the men. A feeling of incredible pride for his mentor swelled up in him, and for reasons he could not understand, he found himself fighting back tears. He carefully wiped them from his eyes while trying to appear that he was merely rubbing fatigue from them.

Dulnear rose to his feet, went over to his fellow northerner, and wrapped his arms around him. At first, Brunnlyn stiffened. His eyes grew large, and he threw his neck back. Then, as if something in his temples had broken, his eyes flooded with tears that began to spill out over his cheeks. The tears were followed by heaving, and his shoulders shook. "Thank you," he wept. "A thousand times, thank you."

Dulnear pulled back, tears now running down his own face. "You must have been incredibly lonely here," he said.

"No," the man answered. "Not after a short time."

"What do you mean?" Dulnear asked.

"You started something, Dulnear," Brunnlyn said. "Something I cannot fully explain. I have discovered that many of us have grown tired of the old ways of endless retaliation."

Dulnear's forehead wrinkled into deep lines and his mouth fell open. "Many of you?" he gasped.

"Yes," Brunnlyn said. "At least a dozen of us have forfeited our hand to follow a new way. We are called the Saor, Brotherhood of Peaceful Warriors."

CHAPTER SEVEN

# WHISPERS IN THE WOODS

Maren followed the tree line along the field that sloped downward toward the Neodrec. The return trip looked much different, since she was journeying on her own two feet instead of being hauled along the trail by the brutish Soeth. She was rehearsing, in her mind, the conversation she was going to have with Faymia when she returned. There was a feeling in her stomach that reminded her of a spinning top just before it fell over. *I don't think they know what blessed means*, she thought. *I am nothing like William*.

There was something about her day spent with the Taalbrem that made her want to cry. Her wobbly stomach spread outward to make a fluttering chest, unusual breathing, and a face that felt like it was vibrating. Eventually, a tear formed in the corner of her eye and she wiped it away with the back of her hand.

As she approached the path that led to the clearing where Soeth grabbed her, she could hear whispers. She stopped, held her breath, and stood motionless for a moment. The whispering sounded heavy and black, and carried a feeling of dread as the breeze delivered the sound to her ears.

Silently, she stepped into the woods and crept inward until she could make out the clearing in the distance. Desiring a sharper view, she climbed a mostly dead pine tree. From midway up the tree, she could see that the voices were coming from Gadoar and Breag, the highground and lowground scouts. "I thought they were enemies," she quietly murmured to herself.

Just then, a snicker erupted between the two men. "I was paid twelve pieces of silver for that information," Gadoar boasted. He had given up whispering and his voice reverberated through the clearing.

"Grand! I receive no less than seven pieces every time I make up some lowground rumor. I've never had it better," Breag claimed.

"Every time I mention war, everyone stops what they're doing to listen. As long as we keep the tribes fighting, you and I are the real chiefs," Gadoar laughed.

Breag chuckled with his highground counterpart. Regaining his composure, he took on a more serious expression and paused for a moment. "You know, a full-on war could decimate what's left of the Ohdium," he observed.

Gadoar joined his companion in contemplating the impact of their goading the tribes to war. "Perhaps it will," he began. "But, by then, I'll be so rich that it won't matter. I can move to Ahmcathare, live in the finest home, and never work another day in my life."

"I suppose," the other scout said. "Besides, our people are resilient. I'm sure they'll rebuild and be just fine."

Maren couldn't believe what she was hearing. The charming, charismatic Gadoar was nothing more than a greedy manipulator. They didn't look evil like Maren imagined evil men to look. It was confusing to her. She thought them both to be decent, kind men. But the words they spoke were dark as pitch and filled her with the desire to be as far away from the Rift as she could get.

Suddenly the dry, gray branch she was standing on snapped and she let out a yelp as she grabbed the trunk of the tree to keep from falling to the ground.

"Who's out there?" Breag shouted, peering beyond the clearing.

Gadoar withdrew a small sword from the sheath at his side. With panic in his eyes, he shrieked, "We can't let anyone know!"

The two scouts walked slowly into the woods. Breag also drew a sword. "Show yourself!" he yelled. "I am the chief's loyal scout. This is an official parley!"

Maren clung to the trunk of the tree as if it were life itself. She knew that any sort of movement could be costly so she squeezed her eyes shut, tried to breathe slowly, and said a prayer.

"I said, this is an official parley!" the man claimed again. "Reveal yourself or be considered an enemy of peace!"

The young girl began to shake. Her arms and shoulders burned with pain from bearing her weight. She tried to get her feet to take some of the load but was afraid of breaking another dead branch, causing the noise to give away her location.

"This is your last chance!" Breag called out. "Come out or we will send soldiers to find and imprison you!"

Gadoar stopped dead in his tracks. Reaching out to touch his co-conspirator's arm, he looked up at Maren's tree. "Well, I'll be!" he shouted. "If it isn't the little dullard who followed me across the neutral zone! Your friend told me she was looking for you. How unfortunate that I found you first!"

"Followed you across the neutral zone?" the Taalbrem scout snorted. "She was just with Le'as getting a tour of the village!"

"Well, you do get around," Gadoar said. His upper lip curled and he moved his sword in a threatening motion over his head. "We'll make sure that your traveling days are over!"

Breag ran to the trunk of the tree. Sheathing his sword, he began to climb it while the other scout stood close by in waiting.

The strength in Maren's arms seemed to be all but gone and she could hear the pounding of her heart throbbing in her ears. Trying desperately to think of a plan, she came up with nothing. All she could do was wait until he reached her, and hope she could hold on long enough to give him a swift kick to his head.

>>>———•———•———

Faymia crouched low with bow drawn. Anxious to release her arrow into the scouts who were terrorizing her friend, she watched and waited for the right moment. She breathed in slowly, and the smell of dead leaves and damp ground filled her nostrils. It was as if the world around her had suddenly become more alive and vibrant.

Seeing her opportunity, she released her bow, sending an arrow through the air and into Gadoar's forearm, causing him to immediately drop his sword to the ground.

"Yeargh!" the man howled, turning his arm over to see the sharp head of an arrow staring up at him.

Just then, Maren realized that she had received what she was waiting for; an opportunity to kick Breag square in the face. As she did he dropped to the ground, landing on his back.

Having lost all strength in her arms, the girl also fell, landing feet-first on the man. An eerie groan wheezed forth from within his chest and he rolled onto his side. She grabbed a nearby stick, holding it like a sword, but her wobbly arm only held it as high as her waist.

Faymia ran as fast as she could to Maren's side, holding her sword ready. "Back away!" she commanded the scouts. "Or the next arrow will find its way through your chest!"

Breag rolled onto his stomach and he clumsily staggered to his feet. Rubbing his shoulder, he joined the other scout and unsheathed his sword. "I'm afraid we can't do that," he declared. "Now neither of you can leave this place."

Unexpectedly, Gadoar grabbed the arrow just below the head and began to tug at it. Grunting like a panting bear, he pulled until it made a complete passage through his arm. He stabbed it into the ground and grabbed his sword. "The man is correct," he said. "I'm afraid you picked the wrong time to take a holiday."

Faymia reached into her tunic with her left hand and retrieved a dagger. She held it with the blade against her forearm and stood so the sword in her right hand was ready to strike. "Let us pass or you will regret it," she warned.

The men laughed in amusement at her threat. "Do you expect us to be frightened by a one-eyed woman and a little girl?" Breag scoffed.

"If I would have wanted it, Gadoar would be dead instead of nursing a wound to his arm," she stated, tightening her grip on her weapons.

Gadoar looked again at his forearm. His nostrils flared and he clenched his jaw. "You were probably aiming for my back," he taunted. "I look forward to giving you what you deserve."

Every one of Faymia's muscles tensed and her mind played out her attacks and defenses. Before she had a chance to take a step forward, Maren was already attacking Breag, beating him senselessly with her stick.

Gadoar swung his weapon above his head and was about to bring it down upon Maren but Faymia leaped forward and blocked his attack. Growling, he kicked the woman in the stomach, sending her to the ground and stomping after her.

Faymia rolled backward and back up to her feet. She swung her sword toward the man's neck but he deflected her blade with his own. Following through with the swing, her blade continued on a downward arc until it struck the side of his right knee.

"Argh!" he cried out but he regained his footing, placing his weight on his left leg. "I'll kill you!" he cried, now flailing his sword with more rage than skill.

A cry rang out from Maren. Wanting to waste no time, Faymia blocked Gadoar's wildly spinning sword, lunged past him, and plunged her knife deep into his right leg. As she did, he crumpled to the ground, cursing.

The woman found Maren knocked to the ground, sitting up holding her right arm. It was bleeding freely as she looked at it in terror. Breag was charging toward her.

Faymia thrust her sword toward the man, missing him, but knocking him back with her shoulder. She was filled with rage at the sight of her friend wounded. "There is no word for the type of scum who would harm a young girl," she seethed.

"The little brat would have fractured my skull!" he retorted. "And I will not let the two of you spoil our plans!"

"Then you can join your newly crippled friend," the woman threatened, and began to advance.

"Wait!" Gadoar cried out. He stumbled to his feet like a newborn horse and hobbled his way over to the other scout. As he did, Faymia crouched beside Maren, helped her up, and handed her the bloody knife.

Leaning against Breag, the man continued. "We will allow you to leave."

Faymia's blood boiled. The two men standing before her made her stomach ill. "I do not need your permission, blackguard!" she hissed. "I can end you both right now and walk out on my own."

Just then, Breag looked at Maren and swallowed hard. The girl was holding the bloody knife in front of her face and taking small steps forward.

When Faymia saw the girl, a deep sense of caution overcame her. She reached forward, placed her hand on Maren's shoulder, and brought her back to her side. She knew that killing these two men would leave a mark on the girl that she would have to live with for the rest of her life.

"Like I said," Gadoar continued. "We will allow you to leave."

"Am I supposed to thank you for your generosity?" Faymia jeered.

"No," the scout said. "You are supposed to make your way north through these woods until you are out of the Ohdium."

The woman was all too happy to think of leaving the Rift. "And what about my horse?" she asked.

"I have no idea where your horse is," he said. "He is probably meandering where you left him. If you can find him before the guard finds you, I suggest you mount up and make haste."

The scout's words echoed slowly through Faymia's mind. "Before the guard finds me?" she asked.

A wicked grin began to crawl from the corner of Gadoar's mouth. "Of course. When I return to my tribe, I will explain how the one-eyed woman and her savage little companion attacked me. You will be hunted and executed if you try to return and report our plans to Thuaid."

Breag laughed and turned toward his partner. "That is brilliant!" he exclaimed. "I'm sure Le'as will reward me for fending off these attackers while scouting for our village."

"You two are despicable," Faymia chided. "Last night, we were attacked. Today, you tried to kill us. And now, you're going to brand us as criminals, just so you can keep milking money and influence out of your people. I don't know how you live with yourselves!"

"We live quite well with ourselves," Gadoar pompously declared. "By the way, you were only attacked because you were in the wrong place at the wrong time. If only one of those rocks would have broken your skull."

"That's right," Breag added. "We had orchestrated a wonderful fight between parties, but there you were with your little mongrel. The world must really dislike you."

Faymia's rising indignation was pierced by the man's words. For a moment, she felt that perhaps the world did dislike her. After all, she was but a former slave, scarred and unfortunate. Attempting to shake the words off, she answered with an assertive, "Go."

"Go?" Breag chortled. "We are the ones setting the terms here, not you."

In a blink, Faymia swept her sword upward, sending the scout's weapon through the air and nearly taking off his littlest finger. Holding the tip of her blade to Gadoar's throat, she repeated, "Go!" Her face was flush with anger as she continued. "Go, or I will kill you both here and now, consequences be damned!"

For a moment there was a hush, and all that could be heard was the breeze. Finally, Breag murmured, "As you say," and began to retrieve his sword.

"Leave it!" the woman commanded, and pressed her blade closer toward Gadoar's neck.

Breag raised his hands in submission and backed away from his sword. Without another word, he began walking west toward the path that led to his village.

Gadoar also raised his hands and stepped backward. "I will enjoy spinning tales of your corruption and violence," he sneered. He then slowly limped his way east toward the Neodrec.

Faymia watched both men until they were out of sight.

When they were, she retrieved the knife from Maren, and the two stood together in silence. Finally, she exhaled a long breath that she didn't realize she was holding. Exhausted, she whispered, "Let's go home."

Maren took Faymia's hand and squeezed. Catching her eyes, she insisted, "No. We have to tell the chiefs."

## CHAPTER EIGHT
# NEWS FROM THE SOUTH

"Now, Son," Dulnear said. He and Brunnlyn stood on either side of the boy with wooden swords drawn. The swords were remarkably accurate reproductions, considering that they were mere tree limbs earlier that morning. The warrior had welcomed the other northerner to camp with them for the night and allowed him to assist in the boy's training that day. "You are surrounded by multiple attackers," he announced. "Their aim is to end your life. What do you do?"

Without a word, Son rolled forward then sprinted sideways, placing Dulnear between himself and Brunnlyn. He swung low, giving his friend a swift strike below the knee, then dashed behind the other warrior, keeping them in a line with each other so they couldn't surround him.

Brunnlyn brought his weapon straight down but the boy dodged out of its way. As he did, he swung his wooden sword backward, striking the large man's hand. Without a second glance he bolted toward the trees, leaving his trainers to rub their wounds.

"Excellent!" Dulnear called out. "If I had two hands, I would applaud you," he joked. He was proud of the boy, and his face beamed with approval.

"Yes, very good," Brunnlyn agreed. "Your mentor has taught you well."

"Thanks," Son grinned. "It helps that this was the twenty-fifth time we've done this drill."

"Ah, yes. We want action and reaction without thought, and this is how we get there," Dulnear explained. "Now, let us try again."

"One moment," Brunnlyn unexpectedly interrupted. He peered into the woods pensively. "Another Saor brother approaches."

Just then a tall, broad figure stepped out of the tree line. He looked harried and exhausted. He hastily approached Brunnlyn.

Dulnear took a sudden step backwards, surprised by his appearance. "Apparently, my secret training place is not so secret," he muttered to Son.

Within seconds, the figure was jogging away and Brunnlyn's countenance went gravely serious. "My apologies for the interruption," he said. "I must tell you something immediately."

Dulnear knew instinctively that something was not right. His eyes narrowed and he swallowed. "What is it?"

Brunnlyn shifted his weight from one leg to another. Clearing his throat, he explained, "The Saor feel that they owe you their lives. When I told you that you have shown us a better way, the gravity of that cannot be exaggerated."

Dulnear felt uncomfortable at the sound of such praise about himself. He glanced at the ground and spoke.

"Thank you for your kind words, but what has you suddenly so concerned?"

"Yes, well," the man continued. "You might say that we have been, um, watching out for you."

"Watching out for me?" Dulnear asked.

"Guarding you, to more accurately put it," Brunnlyn continued. He then added, "And your friends."

Dulnear didn't know what to think. He couldn't believe that a group of northerners had been watching over him, and was disappointed with himself for not noticing. "And why in the world would you believe that I needed guarding?" he asked.

"As I said, we owe you our lives," Brunnlyn said. He then intensified his gaze on Dulnear. "You have made some very powerful enemies," he stated. "And so has your young companion. Have you not wondered why Gale Hill Farm has been left alone since your encounter with the slaver king, Ocmallum?"

Dulnear felt his limbs go cold. He glanced at Son to see his face turn white at the sound of the slaver's name. "We have been bolstering our defenses at Gale Hill since our encounter at Dorcadas," he said. "Are you saying that those slaver scum are planning to attack soon?"

"I am saying that it is fortunate Gale Hill is not a household name, and that slavers have not had an easy time finding it," the man explained. "We have taken out any scouts who have come close, but they are intensifying their efforts."

"Intensifying?" Dulnear croaked. His neck tingled, and his fist coiled tightly around his wooden sword.

"Yes, they have just begun setting up roadblocks,

looking for a northerner traveling with a southern lad," he said. "Ocmallum wants revenge in the worst way, and will exhaust his vast resources to get it."

Dulnear's muscles hardened and he found himself unconsciously swiping his thumb across the jagged pommel of the training weapon. His mind began to formulate the destruction of roadblocks, slavers, and any other lowlife rabble that would seek to harm himself or his friends. "I am afraid that the slaver king will have to learn to live with disappointment then," he said with a low growl.

"But, there is one other very important thing," Brunnlyn added. "Your wife is caught in the middle of a very precarious situation."

Suddenly, the anger in Dulnear's veins turned to surprise. "What? What has happened to Faymia?!"

"There is trouble in the Ohdium Rift," the man said. "War is brewing, and she is in the middle of it. My Saor brother just explained to me that she has been marked as an instigator, and is in danger of being arrested and executed."

"Executed??" Dulnear yelped. "She was taking a holiday. What has happened?"

"Well, it appears that she has acquired your knack for making enemies," Brunnlyn said. "The highground and lowground scouts have been conspiring together to bring their two sides to war. Your wife discovered their plans, so they have spread lies about her so that no one will believe her if she tries to stop it."

The world began to spin around the man from the north. The anger he was feeling shifted to helplessness, and all he could think about was getting down from the mountain to be by Faymia's side. "I cannot believe this!" he declared. "Son, we must break camp as quickly as possible."

The boy was already heading back to the shelter before Dulnear had completed his sentence. Without saying a word, he moved with urgency to pack their things and prepare to leave.

"What will you do?" Brunnlyn asked.

"I will do what I must," he answered. "Starting with leaving for the Ohdium posthaste and finding my beloved." He then paused for a moment and placed his hand on his friend's shoulder. "Come with us," he invited.

Brunnlyn's head shot back in surprise. Taking a deep breath, he replied, "I do not know..."

"Just come with us," Dulnear repeated. "I would be honored to enjoy your company a little longer. Besides, we could use another sword."

The man looked down at the ground. His forehead wrinkled together and his eyes fixed themselves on something in the distance. "I feel far from worthy to take up arms with you. Are you sure?" he asked.

"Absolutely."

Brunnlyn drew another deep breath and exhaled. "Then I will accompany you."

Dulnear tossed aside the wooden weapon and withdrew his sword from its sheath. With steel in his voice he uttered, "Good. Let us ride."

# CHAPTER NINE
# DEAF EARS

Faymia kept her hood over her head. She knew that her eye patch made her recognizable, but taking it off would only draw a different kind of attention. Her only hope was to travel up the ramp that climbed through the Ruhbrem cliffside village without being noticed. She kept her head down and her pace steady, praying that she hadn't made a huge mistake by coming back to warn Thuaid of the scouts' plans.

Moments before, she had rushed to the northern edge of the ravine with Maren. They had found their horse, Addoe, and decided it would be better for the young girl to hide near that place while she hurried back to speak to the chief.

*This is crazy*, Faymia thought to herself. *Why should I care what happens to these people?* Then, she remembered the risk her husband took to purchase her freedom. She recalled that the right thing was seldom the easy thing, and she would struggle to live with herself if she didn't at least try to get word to Thuaid.

As she approached the bookstore, she looked for the old woman who spoke to her that morning. It seemed like weeks had gone by since she had descended that very same path in search of Maren. Unfortunately, there was no blind woman to be found, nor was there even a chair sitting outside of the old dwelling. Knowing that the longer she lingered in one place, the greater chance there was of her being discovered, she kept moving, drawing ever closer to the highest path and the chief's chambers.

Reaching Thuaid's dwelling, Faymia found things to be oddly quiet. She entered through an ornate foyer that had been carved from the black rock of the cliff face. Passing through the foyer and into a broad hallway, she recognized her surroundings from earlier, but they felt very different in the silence.

She navigated her way through torchlit halls, past closed doors and empty rooms until she came to the chief's chamber. The door was ajar, and she could see Thuaid sitting at the head of the large table that she had eaten breakfast at earlier. Candles covered much of the table, and the chandelier was lowered to illuminate the many parchments the chief seemed to be focused on at the moment. Standing next to him was Argach, his assistant.

Faymia sprinted into the room and closed the door behind her. Standing across the table from Thuaid, she pulled back her hood and addressed him. "Sir, I have urgent news."

The man looked up from his work with surprising nonchalance. "Hello there, Faymia," he said. "I'm surprised to see you."

His words were welcoming but his tone felt cold to the

woman. "I'm sorry to disturb you," she began. "But I'm afraid the whole of the Ohdium is in danger."

"Oh?" the chief responded as he raised an eyebrow. "And how can that be?"

"Both the highground and lowground scouts have been conspiring to cause a war," she explained. As she did, the fear that she would be unable to adequately explain what was happening began to stir inside of her. Her voice shook, and her breaths became shallow.

Thuaid gave a subtle glance to his assistant, stood to his feet, and leaned forward with his hands on the table. "Whatever do you mean?"

"I found them in the woods beyond the neutral zone. Gadoar has been lying to you in order to make himself more valuable. He doesn't care about the Ruhbrem, only for the money and influence he gains from stirring fear and uncertainty." Faymia would have continued if not for the strange look she noticed in the man's eyes. She instinctively placed her hand on her sword and placed her left foot behind her.

"Ah, there it is," the chief breathed. "My scout told me that you were a violent firebrand, but I had to see for myself." He then snatched a small, silver bell off the table and quickly rang it. Within seconds, a half dozen guards stormed the room and surrounded her. "Gadoar told me how you attacked him. You put an arrow in his arm, then stabbed him in the leg. He told me you'd be back here, trying to convince me that he was up to no good. I don't know who you think you are, but you're not going to get away with such treachery!"

Faymia looked at Argach for some sort of support. His expression of helplessness told her she wouldn't find any.

"Your misinformation will not go unpunished!" Thuaid added. "Cooperate and go with my guards or they will drag your corpse out. Make the right choice."

Faymia took another step back and considered trying to escape, but the only door was blocked, and she knew an attempt to get back to Maren was futile. As the guards took her weapons from her, she pleaded, "Listen to me! An attack from the Taalbrem is coming! They think they are making a preemptive strike. You must go to their chief and work things out peacefully before your villages are destroyed and your people slain!"

Thuaid stood up straight and puffed out his chest. "The stories people make up," he chided. "Unfortunately for you, I trust my scout completely." He then nodded to the guard nearest Faymia. As the guard placed restraints on her wrists, the chief continued. "Faymia, if that is your name, you are guilty of attempted insurrection. You will be held in the dungeon until the means of your execution have been decided on."

Immediately, panic and regret piled onto Faymia's shoulders. As she was dragged out of the room, images of Maren, Son, and Dulnear flashed through her mind. "Just talk to the lowground chief!" she shouted. "You'll see. Just talk to him!"

CHAPTER TEN

# FEAR AND FRUSTRATION

As Son slung his pack over his shoulder, he gazed into the late-day sky, wondering how they were going to make it down the mountain as the night turned black.

"We will use torches," Dulnear stated, as if he knew what the boy was thinking. He was standing in front of three tree branches that he had driven into the ground. Using a hatchet to split the ends of the branches into quarters, he added, "Brunnlyn is gathering tree pitch."

Son had been listening to his friend and the other northerner plan their rapid journey to the Ohdium Rift. Unfortunately, he missed much of what they had said, since so much of their native language had been sprinkled into the conversation. It was unusual for him to see Dulnear interacting with a fellow countryman, and he found himself feeling a bit on the outside.

When Brunnlyn returned with a tin cup filled with pitch, Dulnear melted it over the fire, then used it to soak pine cones wrapped in fabric. He took the wrapped pine cones and shoved them into the quartered branches to serve as torch heads. Then he lit the torch and handed it to Son. "These should serve us for a while," he said. Then, he did the same for Brunnlyn and himself.

When they were all ready, they headed toward the narrow, zigzagging trail that led down the mountain. As they did, a myriad of thoughts began to fill the boy's mind. He wondered if the horses would still be waiting for them at the bottom. He wondered if they would really make it to the Ohdium in time. And he wondered if all that he had learned over the past few days would be of any use to him.

Occasionally, Son would wake from his fretting to notice that the two northerners had greatly outpaced him and he would have to catch up. The thought of being left behind on the mountain was frightening, especially since the last clinging visions of gray sky had given way to black, and he could only see a very short distance in front of him as his torch flickered.

The night skies in Aun were such that very few people ever traveled after sunset. There was no moon to cast a pale light, nor stars to chart one's course. It gave the boy a feeling of suffocation, and he panicked as the torches of his northern companions grew smaller in the distance. Finally, he yelled, hoping they would slow their steps.

"Dulnear!" he called out, and began running. He tried to keep a light step, focusing on avoiding the many rocks and fallen branches that littered the path. As he did, he glanced and could see that the men's torches had stopped moving. A relief fell over him and he risked a slightly quicker pace.

Suddenly, it felt as if a man had been dropped upon

him from above, knocking him to the ground. At once, he could feel something like daggers tear into his shoulder and tear away the hood from his coat. There was a growl of hot breath and another bite.

Son wailed in terror. His torch had been dropped nearby and he had no clue what was on him. He only knew that the pain was insufferable, and he had to escape or he would die. With his left arm, he tried to keep the deadly maw at bay, and with his right he pulled a dagger from his belt and began stabbing at the neck of the beast. It let loose a terrifying howl and leapt back.

The boy tried to scramble to his feet, but his injured body denied him. He held up his knife, planning to sink it deep into the animal if it attacked him again. The creature released a roar and Son's body went limp with fear. He strained desperately to see its form, hoping he would be able to roll out of the way if it pounced. As he did, he noticed a warm light grow from behind him as Dulnear and Brunnlyn rushed up the trail. Because of their torches, he could make out the shape of an enormous cat on its haunches, poised to strike.

A torch flew over him, landing at the beast's feet. Then the northerners sped by, hemming it in. Dulnear brought his sword down hard upon the shoulder of the animal. It seemed to be more enraged than injured and swiped its great claws at the man, nearly catching his neck.

Brunnlyn kicked the monster hard and, when it turned its attention toward him, he shoved his torch in its eyes. It let loose a blood-curdling wail and spun around, knocking him over with its hind end. As it did, Dulnear swiped upward with his blade, catching its chest and inflicting a modest gash.

Suddenly, the giant let loose a roar that filled every part of the night air. Son felt his body vibrate from the sound and watched in awe as it leaped over him and into the darkness.

The boy tried to catch his breath as Dulnear and Brunnlyn collected the still-burning torches. Trembling, he asked, "What was that?"

"A kottur," his friend answered. "The largest I have ever seen. And, in this darkness, I do not know if it is near or far."

"I have never been so close to one," Brunnlyn added. "It could have taken your head clean off, boy."

Son shuddered at the thought of being eaten by the beast. He tried again to get to his feet but his entire body radiated with agony. "I can't get up," he groaned.

Dulnear sheathed his weapon and turned to assist the boy. As he did, the ground shook. Stopping in his tracks, he whispered, "I think I know why the kottur fled, and it was not because of my sword."

"Rockfall," the other northerner announced. "Get against the mountain!"

Abandoning any gentleness, Dulnear grabbed Son by the front of his coat, threw his arm around him, and dashed toward the side of the trail nearest the mountainside. As he did, rocks began to roll down from above, pelting them as they tumbled through the lightless night air.

The three pressed themselves against a boulder embedded in the slope. Jagged stones, both large and small, showered down. Wrapped in the arms of his large friend,

Son could feel a rock strike the man from time to time. The horror of the moment was made even worse by the fact that he could not see his hand in front of his face, since the torches were snuffed out by falling debris.

Then, just as quickly as it had begun, the avalanche ceased. "Are you all right?" Son asked Dulnear.

"I will be," the northerner answered. "Can you stand?"

"I'll try," Son said, and he stood on his feet as Dulnear lowered him to the ground. When he found that his footing was stable, he stated, "That's the second time you've saved me from a rockslide. I think we should stay away from mountains for a while."

Quietly snickering, the man replied, "Indeed." He then asked into the air, "Are you all right, Brunnlyn?"

The other northerner sounded weak. With a breathy voice he answered, "A few strikes, but I will recover." He then added, "One thing is for sure. Our descent will have to wait until daylight."

>>>———•———➤

The air was dank and the stone floor was unforgiving as Faymia rested her head upon it. The dungeon was in the furthest part of Thuaid's dwelling, carved deep into the side of the Rift. The fatigue in her body told her it was the middle of the night but, for all she knew, it could have been the next afternoon. She had been served no food, and had not slept. There were no lanterns or torches to illuminate her surroundings. There was only pure darkness and the damp smell in the air.

*I had more freedom as a slave than I've had in this place,* she thought to herself. It was difficult to remember all of the good that had come into her life as she lay there, staring into the black. Her surroundings seemed to erase from her mind the blessings until there was nothing left but weariness of heart and thought.

*Futility*, she thought. She began to consider that it was futile to help others. After all, they're just going to believe whatever they think most plausible. She began to reckon that people don't change, grow, or improve. They only do what is easiest, even if it's at the expense of peace and unity.

The darkness of her surroundings seeped into her until hoping felt like a silly idea. Since there was no point in anticipating a favorable outcome, she closed her eyes to sleep.

Just as she began to drift off, there was a faint scratching somewhere in the cell. *And now there's a rat in here with me*, she thought, springing her eyes open. *If I go to sleep now, I may wake up to it gnawing at me.*

She clapped her hands, hoping the sudden sound would scare off the rat. There was silence and she closed her eyes again. As she did, the distant sound of a voice could be heard in her mind as she traveled from waking to sleeping. The voice grew nearer and the darkness dissipated into the sight of Gale Hill Farm, and her husband. He looked lovingly at her and spoke, but all that could be heard was scratching.

Faymia's heavy eyes opened again, then closed. The scratching seemed to be coming from her left, so she rolled and smacked her right hand against the floor. This time, the noise stopped for only a moment, then continued, but now sounded like it was coming from a short distance beyond where her feet were laying.

Letting out an audible groan, she rolled her back onto the floor again and clapped her hands a few more times, hoping she could quickly fall asleep so deeply that the noise would not wake her. The noise paused and she placed her hands behind her head.

*If I'm eaten by rats, I'm eaten by rats*, she thought to herself. *At least these people would be denied the satisfaction of executing me*. She then breathed deeply and began to drift off as she released a long sigh.

Once again the voice echoed in her mind and her husband's face appeared. He spoke kind words to her and her dream-self wept. "What am I supposed to do?" she asked Dulnear.

"I do not know," he replied. "I only know what you are *not* supposed to do."

"And what is that?" she asked.

"You are not supposed to give up."

Faymia let those words echo through her soul. She remembered her husband's stubborn grip on hope and wondered aloud, "But these people seem determined to deny the truth. How am I supposed to hope?"

"It is not a matter of how," Dulnear answered. "And it is not a matter of optimistic feelings. You either hold onto hope or you let it go."

Faymia was fully aware that she was dreaming and that her physical self was lying on a cold dungeon floor. She wrestled with the words of her husband. As she did, his image faded away and she restlessly slept to the sound of clawing and scratching nearby.

Dulnear felt the back of his head. It was damp with blood and throbbed to the beating of his heart. He spotted a still-lit torch nearby and walked over to retrieve it. "Sit," he told his companions.

He held out the torch and tried to gauge how his surroundings had changed from the rockslide. It was difficult in the darkness, and the ground itself felt different beneath his feet. Regardless, he knew that if he continued to work his way downward, he would eventually reach his destination, and that fact kept a feeling of desperation from overtaking him.

"Faymia," he whispered to himself and rejoined Son and Brunnlyn, who were seated on the ground, leaning against the side of the mountain.

"Did you find the other torches?" the boy asked.

"Unfortunately, I only found this one," he answered. "How are you recovering?"

"I think I'll be fine," Son said. "That beast gave me quite the scare." He then gently moved his legs as if trying to decide if they still worked.

Turning toward his countryman, Dulnear asked, "And how about you, my friend?"

There was no answer from the northerner, and it was too dark to tell if he was moving.

Dulnear waited a moment and asked again, "Brunnlyn, are you all right?"

Still, only silence came from the man.

"Brunnlyn!" Dulnear shouted.

"Stop yelling," Brunnlyn croaked. "I am sleeping."

Dulnear wanted to growl something in anger, but found himself laughing instead. "You had me worried there for a moment."

"For what?" Brunnlyn replied. "Being attacked by a kottur and facing a landslide is just another day in Tuasarum. Besides, us northerners recover quickly."

Dulnear knew his friend had the right idea. Not stopping to rest would not be wise. He sat down beside his companions and closed his eyes. "We shall rest for just a moment," he said. "But then we must complete our descent."

In his mind, the man from the north imagined being reunited with his beloved Faymia. The thought strengthened him, but he did not allow himself to fall into a deep sleep for fear that he would sleep too long and not make it to her in time.

>>>————•————⪥

Dulnear carefully led his friends around fallen rocks and broken sections of the winding trail. It was an infuriatingly slow trek. Between the many obstacles, having only one torch, and the slow pace that his injured friends were moving, he struggled to keep his thoughts from drifting to grim places.

"How far along do you think we are?" Son asked from behind the lumbering Brunnlyn.

"I reckon we should be reaching the foot of the mountain by daybreak," the man answered. "But there is no telling what lies in our path further down."

Suddenly, a sound that sent daggers of ice into them

reverberated through the air. They froze in unison, and Dulnear quickly handed the torch to his fellow northerner so he could withdraw his sword.

"The kottur has returned," Brunnlyn announced. "And he sounds to be dangerously near."

Again, a terrifying howl rang out. Dulnear tried to determine which direction it came from and a ringing began in his ears, making the effort more difficult. "Do not make a sound," he instructed. He then sheathed his sword and took the torch back from the other northerner.

Finally, he took three steps forward, then held the light to his left, illuminating the giant cat's fierce face. It let loose a massive roar but, to Dulnear's surprise, it did not attack.

"Kill it!" Son yelled out as he drew his weapon. "It's probably back for the rest of my shoulder!"

"Stay back!" Dulnear ordered. As his eyes adjusted, he noticed that one of the beast's hind legs was crushed by a boulder. "He cannot harm us."

"Then let us be on our way," Brunnlyn suggested.

Dulnear continued to examine the kottur. It was pinned down by the rock, and would most assuredly die there. There was something about the animal that caused the man to swell with pity, even in the midst of desperately trying to reach Faymia. "We must free it," he said.

"What?!" Son cried out. "That thing almost ate me whole!"

"It was hungry," Dulnear explained. "And I am sure you looked like a delicious snack." He then reached into his bag and took out some dried meat he had prepared for the journey home. Holding it out to the beast, he said, "Here you go, old kottur."

The animal sniffed the meat, then licked it. Making a deep purring sound, it took it from the northerner's hand and quickly chewed it up.

"Now, quickly, let us roll this stone off its leg," he said.

"What if it attacks?" the boy asked.

"In this state, I do not think it would be much of a match for the three of us," Dulnear answered.

Reluctantly, Brunnlyn and Son joined Dulnear at the hind quarters of the animal. As they did, it breathed a low growl and weakly raised its upper lip, exposing fangs that still had meat caught between them.

"What do we do now?" Brunnlyn asked. "The moment we roll this stone, the monster will reach back and attack."

Dulnear rubbed his chin and thought. "Now, lads," he began. "Brunnlyn and I will roll the stone. We will push downhill, so it should be fairly easy. Son, you will stand behind us with your sword just in case it attacks."

"No way!" the boy protested. "I'm still bleeding from the last time it mauled me. That thing is dangerous!"

"It really is," Brunnlyn added. "Perhaps we should just be thankful that it is not lurking in the dark waiting to feast on our entrails."

Dulnear knew the others were right. It was not wise to test one's luck in such a way. However, he could not deny the compassion he felt for the beast. Something inside of him was telling him to help it. "You are both correct," he said. "It is completely unreasonable to believe the animal would behave outside its nature. But I feel the need to free it whether you help me or not."

Son and Brunnlyn stood and stared at the man in disbelief. Finally, the boy sighed and walked over to his friend. "What do you want me to do?"

"Just keep your back to mine and be ready to strike the animal, if need be," Dulnear explained. He then directed his attention toward Brunnlyn. "Will you help me?"

His fellow northerner sighed, then joined him near the boulder and muttered, "You are even more mad than I thought. Let us do this."

"Get ready," Dulnear began. "On three, we push."

The two men both pressed their right shoulders against the rock and firmly pushed with their left hands. "Mad as a hatter," Brunnlyn added.

"One, two, three!" Dulnear exclaimed. The two of them heaved with all their might, grunting as they did. As the stone began to tilt forward, the giant cat began kicking its legs. Startled, Brunnlyn released his hold momentarily. "Brunnlyn!!" the man from the north boomed, struggling to keep the object from falling back down.

Immediately, the other northerner repositioned himself and began pushing again. Grunting, they drove the stone until it rolled off the trail and down the mountain slope.

"Dulnear!" Son called out as the animal sprang to its feet. "He's coming back for seconds!"

The man grabbed the boy by the back of his coat and yanked him closer. He then withdrew his sword as Brunnlyn did the same. "Stay calm," he said.

The kottur roared into the pitch-black sky, and Dulnear began to wonder if he hadn't made a grave mistake. He moved Son behind him with his right arm and tightened his grip on his sword.

The beast shook its head and breathed a strange growl,

then unexpectedly turned away from the travelers and limped off into the darkness.

Dulnear pushed another stone from the path while doing his best to illuminate where they were stepping. His thoughts wrestled over the wisdom of freeing the animal, and hoped that taking the time to do so did not put his wife in any further danger.

"Watch your step," he warned as he waved the torch over a rock that covered most of the trail. He had journeyed up and down the mountain many times before. He knew exactly how long the route took to travel in normal conditions, and was frustrated that they were forced to move at such a slow pace.

After they had toiled much, the mountain trail began to slope more gradually and the rocks became fewer and further between. Tall pines stood on either side of the trail and the air felt richer. "Listen," he said, slightly picking up his pace.

"What is it?" Son asked, trying to match Dulnear's stride.

Answering for his fellow northerner, Brunnlyn chimed, "Crickets. We are approaching the foot of the mountain. And birds are singing. The sky will be growing light soon."

Dulnear's tired heart began to lighten at the thought of reaching the horses, but his eyes burned and his wounds began to throb anew. "Almost there," he said, more to himself than to the others.

Soon, the forest opened up to grasslands. They formed

a blanket over the ground as its gradual slope flattened into the distance. The blackness of the sky gave way to a dark gray. Tired of carrying the torch, the man from the north put it out and tossed it aside.

As the trail emptied out into the endless field, Dulnear could see broken lines of grass where the horses had been feeding. Comforted by the fact that they were probably nearby, he kept moving further afield until they came upon a high patch of ground where little grass grew.

The three stood in the small clearing and looked outward. It was strangely quiet there, and the stillness felt unnatural after a night of troublesome travel. Peering east, Dulnear could see the backs of their horses moving slowly above the tall grass. He whistled and they lifted their heads to glance in his direction. Brunnlyn also whistled and smiled when he saw his steed in the distance with the others.

Dulnear's body felt heavy, as if gravity had suddenly taken on greater weight. He sat down and closed his eyes, but the sense of moving down the mountainside still lingered. "I am going to rest while we wait for the horses," he announced. "It may be the last chance we have to do so before we reach the Ohdium." He then lay back and rested his head upon his right forearm.

Brunnlyn looked out and whistled one more time. Then, without saying a word, he joined his friend in reclining upon the ground. Son did the same, and the three of them formed a circle in the clearing.

Dulnear briefly opened his eyes to gauge how far along the new morning was. There was a tension inside of him between resting and hurrying south to reach Faymia. Everything in him wanted to keep moving, but his weary eyes overpowered his will and they closed. Hoping he would awaken the moment the horses reached the patch of high ground, he drifted off into a reluctant slumber.

The sensation of flying quickly over meandering roads and rolling hills filled Dulnear's body. He was moving so fast that the surrounding countryside was a blur in his peripheral vision.

Suddenly, a massive ravine with cliff dwellings to his left and rolling forest to his right stood before him. He felt great comfort in knowing that he had arrived at the Rift. That comfort was quickly replaced by a sense of panic as he searched for Faymia but couldn't find her.

"Faymia!" the man cried out. "Faymia, where are you?"

Riding across the neutral zone, he continued to call out but received no answer. Not only was his love nowhere to be found, but the Ohdium was completely vacant. Scanning the cliff dwellings above, he asked himself aloud, "Did I come to the wrong place?"

As he continued to search, he noticed an odor begin to fill his nostrils. It was foul, like rotting flesh mixed with wet animal. In the distance, he could hear the sound of horses neighing in panic. He looked around and saw neither the source of the odor nor the anxious horses.

Then, it felt as if a soggy whetstone was being dragged across his face and the stench intensified. After rubbing his face, he smelled his hand. It was covered in a putrid odor that made him gag.

"Dulnear!" he heard someone call out. "Dulnear, open your eyes!" the voice called out again.

The man from the north came to the realization that he was dreaming, and he willed his eyelids to open.

As his exhausted eyes grew clearer, he saw that he was lying on his side, face-to-face with the enormous kottur. It was on its side as well, with one paw draped across the man's ribs. Stifling a startled gasp, he looked up to see Brunnlyn stealthily approaching the beast from behind, ready to plunge his sword into it.

"Step back," Dulnear whispered. "If you fail to kill it, it will only become enraged and maul me to death."

The animal yawned, and immediately Dulnear realized the origin of the horrible smell in his dream. "Your breath is the worst I have ever smelled," he said in a low, kind voice to the animal. He then gently moved its paw away from him and slowly climbed to his feet.

The creature followed suit and, as it did, it swiped the side of its snout against Dulnear's chest.

The man from the north stood there in disbelief. "Are you two seeing this?" he asked.

"I'm seeing it, but I don't believe it," Son answered, taking a small step backwards.

"I believe it has taken a liking to you. I have never in all my life seen anything like it," Brunnlyn added.

Dulnear was shaken by the affection of the animal. He worried that its seemingly friendly attention could instantly turn into a violent attack, and that concern stayed at the front of his mind. He took a deep breath and haltingly reached out to scratch behind its ears. As he did, the kottur rubbed its head against Dulnear's arm.

"Get the horses ready," he said to his companions in a quiet voice.

As Son calmed the anxious horses and prepared them to leave, Brunnlyn continued to keep an eye on the kottur, preparing to strike if need be.

"Perhaps it is grateful that we set it free," Brunnlyn observed.

"Or maybe I smell particularly delicious," Dulnear added. "Either way, we must make haste to the Rift or risk losing Faymia."

The huge beast then made a low, rumbling noise, lowered itself to the ground, and rolled onto its back, moving its shoulders back and forth.

"Disgusting," Brunnlyn grunted. "I think it wants you to rub its mangy belly."

Looking down and stroking the animal's lush bib, Dulnear smiled tentatively. "So, we are friends now, eh?" he said. After examining it, he looked up to his fellow northerner and announced, "It is a nursing female. It is likely that she was protecting her cubs last night."

"And they did not survive the earthslide," Brunnlyn added.

"You poor thing," Dulnear consoled as he continued to pet the animal. It then shifted onto its side and closed its eyes. He reached into his bag and took out the remaining dried meat he had stored there. "Give me what rations you have," he instructed both of his companions.

Son and Brunnlyn glanced at each other, brought their food over, and Dulnear laid it in front of the kottur's mouth. It sniffed the meat, gave it a taste, and began eating it.

"Now, while she is busy with breakfast, let us quickly ride on," he said.

The three of them scrambled to their horses and began to trot away at a pace Dulnear hoped would not prompt the animal to jump up and pursue. Looking back, he felt pity for the creature, but hoped to never see it again.

## CHAPTER ELEVEN
# FRAGILE FREEDOM

"Faymia," a small voice whispered. "Wake up. We don't have much time."

The woman opened her eyes to see the silhouette of a young girl she immediately recognized to be Maren. Turning her head, she could see a faint light flickering outside the open door to her cell. "Maren, how did you get in here?" she asked. Her entire body felt as if she had been jolted from one world to another, and she wasn't completely certain it wasn't a dream.

"I've been scraping at the mortar around the bolt all night," the girl explained. "By the way, thank you for the encouraging applause. Unfortunately, it would draw the attention of the guards and I would have to stop and hide until it became quiet again."

Faymia was dumbfounded. Feeling silly, she admitted, "I thought a rat was scratching nearby and I was trying to scare it away."

"That doesn't make any sense," Maren observed. She then handed the woman a large knife and said, "The chief is in his chambers, and something terrible is brewing. If we're going to talk with him, it has to be now."

Faymia deeply admired the faith of the young girl, and wished her own was as great. She sat up and shook the cobwebs from her head. "Has the war begun?"

"I don't know," Maren said. "But before sneaking into Thuaid's dwelling, I could see torches being placed along the center of the Neodrec. Perhaps they mean to do away with the neutral zone."

Standing to her feet, Faymia asked, "Is it possible for us to get past the guards and to the chief's chamber?"

"Possibly. They have a very small security crew now," Maren said. "I think most of them are gathered at the bottom of the walkway, preparing to defend the village."

"Then it might be possible to get to Thuaid, and once more try to talk some sense into him before swords are drawn," the woman deduced. She then made her way to the door.

"Wait, listen!" Maren interrupted with an urgent whisper.

The sound of footsteps could be heard echoing down the long, torchlit hallway. Immediately, Faymia closed the door. "On the floor, in front of the door," she instructed the girl. She then dashed toward the opposite wall and sat down.

The outline of a man's face appeared in the barred window at the top of the door. "You in there," he called out. "Looks like the chief is going to wait to execute you. Most of the men have been called to the Neodrec." He then added, "But you can rot in here for all I care."

Faymia prayed that the man wouldn't put too much

weight on the door, and that Maren leaning against it would be enough to keep it from jostling and indicating that it was no longer locked. She hung her head and did her best to appear weakened and despairing. "Thirsty," she groaned. "Please, water."

The guard maliciously brayed through the window. "Thirsty, are ye?" he snorted. "Well that's too bad." He then wrinkled his nose in disgust and walked away.

When the woman decided that he was beyond earshot, she crawled over to her friend. "That was close," she breathed. "We have to get out of here. How in the world did you get here anyway?"

"I'm small," the young girl said matter-of-factly. "And there are lots of dark corners to hide in when the guards aren't paying attention." Then she added, "But you're too big for that."

Faymia pushed aside the assumption that the child was making a statement about her weight and thought for a moment. She knew they would most likely have to fight their way to the chief, and the act of doing so would only cast a poor light on their attempt to promote peace. Knowing she had to take the risk, she asked, "Are you ready for a tussle?"

Maren swallowed and began massaging her ear. "Sure," she croaked. "Let's do it."

"All right, I'm going to open the door. You get on your hands and knees behind me and don't move until I say."

As the girl followed her instructions, Faymia took a deep breath and slowly opened the door to her cell.

"Yoo-hoo!" Faymia called out into the dimly lit hallway. She was standing in the doorway with the door flung completely open. "Mister guard, where'd you go?"

The woman paused and braced herself for the rush of an angry guard but there was nothing.

"HELLO!" she called out again. "Come back here, you big ninnyhammer."

Maren giggled at Faymia's insult. "You big ninnyhammer," she whispered to herself.

The woman let out a, "Shhhh." Then she added, "You must be completely silent for this to work."

"Sorry," the young girl apologized, then silently mouthed the word, "Ninnyhammer."

Continuing, Faymia shouted, "Hey, cumberworld! Come back here!" She then stood and waited some more. Wondering if the man had left the dwelling, she leaned her shoulder against the doorway.

Finally, the sound of a single set of feet could be heard approaching from down the hall. "You're going to pay for those words!" the guard shouted. When he was close enough to see that the woman was standing with her cell door open, he began to run. "Hey!" was all he could get out as he withdrew his sword and charged.

"Come and get me, you inept turd!" Faymia taunted.

The man picked up speed, huffing and puffing down the hall. Raising his sword, he retorted, "I'll show you who the turd is!"

Faymia stood her ground, resisting the urge to move aside too soon. With one last goad, she yelled, "Fopdoodle!!"

"Ahhhh!" the guard screamed, barreling toward her.

At the very last second, Faymia stepped backward past the doorway, then sideways into the cell, causing the man to trip over Maren's curled-up form. He flew through the air, smashing his head against the back wall.

Immediately, Maren jumped up and began kicking the guard savagely. "Ninnyhammer!" she shouted.

"Wait, he's out!" Faymia interrupted. Observing the man, she could see that he was completely unconscious. She then unfastened his sword belt and strapped it around her own waist.

"A blackjack!" Maren chirped, pointing toward an object that looked like the handle of a sword. It was wrapped in leather and had a strap attached to its end.

Faymia took the weighty weapon from the guard and added, "This should come in handy." She then secured the strap around her wrist, holding tightly to the blunt object's grip.

"What are you going to do?" Maren asked.

Faymia clenched her teeth and faced the door. "Knock out some guards. Then maybe knock out the chief if he refuses to listen to reason."

>>> ⸻ ⦁ ⸺

"Wait here," Faymia told Maren. "When you hear me tap the club against the wall three times, then come to me."

"All right," Maren agreed, tugging at her ear.

"Just to be sure, like this," the woman continued. She then slowly tapped the blackjack against the wall outside her cell three times.

"I get it," Maren responded shortly.

Faymia was nervous about leaving the girl so close to the unconscious guard. She handed her back the knife she used to scrape away the mortar around the door's latch. "All right, take this. Hopefully, you won't need it." She was about to turn around and head down the hallway when she stopped, got down on one knee, and gave the girl a hug. It was something she realized she should have done earlier. "Thank you for coming for me."

"You're welcome," Maren answered, and squeezed the woman's neck. "Now, go get that ninnyhammer."

Faymia grinned at the girl and gave her one more squeeze. She stood tall, took a deep breath, and turned to head down the torchlit hallway. After taking a few broad steps, she stopped and listened. She could only hear one set of footsteps in the distance. She reckoned that whoever it was must have been too preoccupied to notice or care that the first guard hadn't returned yet.

When the hallway came to an end, it emptied into a space where she could go either left or right. Noticing that the footsteps were coming from the passage leading right, she pressed her back against the wall so anyone coming from that direction wouldn't immediately see her. Doing her best to impersonate a male voice, she cleared her throat and croaked, "Hey...guy."

The footsteps seemed to be getting neither closer nor further away so she peered around the corner to get a better idea of how far away the guard was. The only thing she could see was a vague shadow that appeared to be pacing over a small area.

"Hey!" she yelled down the hall. "You better get over

here!" *I'm not very good at this*, she thought to herself as she listened for the guard to come.

Faymia noticed the footsteps were now moving in her direction. As they drew closer, they sped up to a jog. She took a small step back and held the blackjack above her head, ready to strike. As the man turned the corner, she brought the blunt object down, striking his temple. For a moment, he stood there with a surprised expression, then crumpled to the floor.

The woman tapped the club against the wall three times and very soon after, Maren came running to her. The girl looked at her, then down to the fallen guard. "Another blackjack!" she declared, and she took it from the man's belt.

Faymia noticed Maren was wearing her eye patch again and she held the weapon in the same manner as herself. She hoped the influence she had on the young girl was a good one, and one day they could find themselves living with more routine and less adventure. "All right, which way?" she asked.

"Down that way," Maren said as she pointed toward the righthand passage.

"All right, wait here for my signal," Faymia instructed, and slowly started in the direction the last guard had come from.

Further down the hallway, another passage opened up leading to the right. Not knowing whether to keep going straight or take the right passage, she stopped again to listen. Breaking the silence, a guard began coughing. The noise rang clearly from the hall going to the right.

Faymia waited to make sure she didn't hear any additional guards, then tiptoed back to the nearest torch and took it off the wall. She tossed it onto the floor where the two passageways met and yelled, "Fire! Get over here!" Then she waited out of sight with her club raised to knock the man on the head.

The guard ran over and bent down to grab the torch. As he did, Faymia brought the weapon down on the back of his head.

A deep growl gushed forth from the guard and he jolted upright, rubbing his head. He was much larger than the woman anticipated, and she stepped back.

"How did you get out of your cell?" the man grunted.

Without responding, Faymia turned to run back the way she came. But before she could get far, the ogreish man had her by the back of her tunic. He yanked her toward himself and shoved her against the wall. "I think it may be a good time for your execution after all," he jeered, and reached for his sword.

A thud suddenly sounded in the hallway and the guard yelped in pain.

"Hand!" Maren shouted, appearing from nowhere, holding up her new blackjack.

Before the man even had a chance to process the presence of a strange child suddenly before him, the girl hit him on the shin, causing him to groan and grab at his leg. Faymia spun around to the back of the man and kicked him square in the back, sending his head against the wall.

The guard turned around, appearing partially disoriented but growing more furious by the moment. This time, he successfully retrieved his sword and cocked his arm back to strike. Pushing Maren aside, he took a step closer toward

Faymia. Just as he brought his sword down she rolled out of the way, withdrew the sword she had taken from the first guard, and countered his attack by swiping at his side.

The brutish man blocked the blow and trapped Faymia's sword under his arm. With a wicked grin he stepped forward, closing the distance between the two of them. The woman struggled to regain control of her sword and knew she was close to being pinned against the wall, defenseless.

"Yeargh!" the man bellowed as Maren forced the large, dull knife into the back of his leg.

As the man dropped down onto one knee, he swung a huge fist backward, almost hitting Maren. As he did, Faymia came down on his left shoulder with her blade. He dropped his sword and clutched the gash, shouting obscenities.

Before he had a chance to recover, Maren had climbed onto his right shoulder and began bashing him on the head with her blackjack. Then, Faymia joined in with hers. With each blow, the man grew dizzier. Eventually, he fell face-forward and Maren leaped to the floor before being pinned underneath him.

The two stood there and watched him for a moment. "Don't get up," Faymia said quietly to herself. She then turned to Maren and said, "I told you to wait for my signal."

"I know," the girl replied. "But it sounded like you needed help."

The woman sighed. She knew Maren was right, and there was no time to debate. "Well, I hope that was the last one. This is taking longer than I'd hoped."

"It is," Maren informed. "The chief's chamber is down this hall to the right."

Faymia took a deep breath and mustered the strength and courage to continue. "Then let's go," she said as she sheathed her sword and stashed the blackjack in her belt.

>>>———•———→

Faymia slowly opened the door to Thuaid's chambers. As before, he was sitting at the head of the large table. Only this time, he was dressed for battle. He was writing on a long parchment, and his eyes were filled with intensity.

"Sir, please listen," the woman implored as she approached the table. "While there is still a chance."

The chief's red eyes went wide with surprise and he sprang to his feet with his hand on his sword. "How did you get out of your cell?!" he barked.

Just then, Maren came in and stood next to Faymia. She was clutching the blackjack, and stared at the man with grim seriousness.

"Never mind," Thuaid scowled, partially rolling his eyes. "I see you had help."

"I don't mean any disrespect, sir. The war you are preparing for can still be avoided," Faymia beseeched. "It's not too late. You can still meet with the lowground chief and avoid bloodshed."

Thuaid peered at the woman, then at Maren. "You two do not look like ones who avoid bloodshed. Why do you care what happens here in the Ruhbrem?"

Faymia thought for a moment. There were many good reasons why she believed war should be avoided. However, she reckoned the chief would not be moved by any of them. Finally, she blurted out, "Because life matters."

Thuaid crossed his arms and shook his head. "That's it? Did you find that in a book of cliches?"

The woman bit down and exhaled. The fact that the chief had not called for his guards yet was a sign he was willing to listen. However, he was still very resistant to a parley with the Taalbrem chief. She swallowed and said, "Because you are wiser than this." She hoped boldness would fare better than the meekness she had been displaying. "Because being manipulated by an attention-seeking, opportunist of a scout is beneath you."

For the first time, Thuaid's veneer began to crack. He looked down for a moment, then back toward Faymia. "If I even consider what you're saying, I'd look like a fool," he began. "I have already sent men to hold the line across the Neodrec. If I meet with Le'as, then I'll have to admit I was duped by Gadoar. I will never have the respect of my people again."

"You will have no people left to pay you respect if you go to war!" the woman warned. "Only misery and heartbreak. The future of your people should be more valuable than appearing right!"

"You don't know!" the chief retorted. "Leadership is more than doing what you feel is right. I cannot appear weak, or uncertain, or indecisive."

"You mean you can't admit you were wrong and change course!" Faymia added.

"Look, I've had just about enough of you!" Thuaid boomed. His face turned crimson and his eyes peered forcefully.

The room fell silent, and Faymia imagined herself staring in at the conversation from a distance. She wondered what to say next, hoping it would restore the chief's openness to talk. Then, the small voice of Maren could be heard.

"The taek," the young girl said, taking a modest step forward.

"What?" Thuaid stumbled. "What did you say?"

"The taek," Maren repeated. "That is the reason you should reconsider. There will never be more beautiful carvings as long as you are divided."

The chief looked around the room. His eyes grew wide and wistful, as if all of the beautifully ornate carvings in the walls and furnishings had been gone for decades and suddenly returned. "It is true we have lost much in our separation," he mourned. "But coming back together as one people is easier said than done."

Suddenly, the three guards Faymia and Maren had disposed of came bursting in the room, led by the largest one, swinging his sword wildly.

Faymia leaped to the top of the table and withdrew the sword she had stolen. She blocked the attack and chopped downward onto the man's shoulder wound she had recently inflicted.

The man howled, sounding like an animal releasing its death moan. He dropped his sword and backed away from the table, stumbling backwards.

The second guard then ran to the table, swiping at Faymia's legs. He yelped in pain as Maren unexpectedly bashed at his shins from under the table. Taking advantage of the distraction, the woman thrust her sword into the man's right arm. He also dropped his sword and took a step backward.

The guard who was previously left in the dungeon cell tentatively stepped forward and retrieved the large guard's sword from the floor. Until this point, he was weaponless, since Faymia was holding his sword and blackjack. "Don't worry, I'll put an end to this, sir," he declared to the chief.

Maren crouched further under the table. She could be heard whispering, "Shin shatters are all that matters."

Faymia reinforced her stance, ready to incapacitate the man.

"Stop!" the chief shouted, and the swirling room came to a standstill. Addressing the guards, he ordered, "Leave us."

"But, sir..." the first guard muttered. "She is a dangerous instigator."

"Do as I say!" Thuaid commanded.

The guard turned and helped the other two to their feet, and they made their way toward the door.

"Take them to the infirmary, and prepare to go to the Neodrec," the chief added. Turning to Faymia, he said, "No one is going to harm you. Please get down off my table."

The woman lowered herself to the floor. As she did, Maren joined her at her side. The room felt still and tense as she surveyed the man, hoping to find a change in his countenance. "Please," she called once more.

Thuaid scratched at his elbow and glanced around the room. Spotting a small table against the west wall, his eyebrow raised and he walked over to it. When he returned, he was holding Faymia's bow and sword. He set them on the large table before her and said, "These belong to you. Weapons of such beauty should not be left here to gather dust." He then returned to the head of the table and began to write something on a parchment.

Faymia removed the stolen belt from her waist and gathered her belongings, but not before stashing the black-jack beneath her tunic. As hope began to rise inside her, she asked, "Does this mean...?"

"This means I want you to leave," the chief answered abruptly. "You are free to go, but only if you promise never to return to the Ruhbrem." He then folded the parchment he had just been writing on, slid it into an envelope, and placed his seal upon it. Handing it to her, he added, "This letter will grant you safe passage. However, it is dated for today only. If you try to come back, you will be arrested, and you will be executed."

Faymia felt her hope quickly deflate as she took the letter. Holding it tightly, she stared at the chief, longing to say or do something that would make him consider calling a truce. All she could say was, "You do not know what you are doing," and she turned to leave with Maren in tow.

The two made their way through the black stone halls of the chief's dwelling, and finally approached the passage to the walkway that led down to the neutral zone. As they drew closer, they could hear the growing sound of hostile men shouting, banging their fists against armored chests and goading each other on.

CHAPTER TWELVE

# BLOCKADE

S on, Dulnear, and Brunnlyn rode their horses hard
through winding, rolling country. Southward they
flew, past the great city of Ahmcathare and the
surrounding villages, stopping only once to water the
horses.

The boy watched the two northerners ride with faces of
stone. They exuded a strength and confidence he deeply
desired to have one day. He hoped that when they arrived at
the Ohdium Rift he could be of some use.

Unexpectedly, Dulnear held up his iron hand and
slowed the pace of his horse to a trot, and Brunnlyn
followed suit. Not yet knowing why they were slowing
down, Son did the same.

"What is it?" the boy asked. It seemed odd, since the
nearest village was a ways back, and there was nothing but
hedges and stone walls on either side of them.

"Up ahead," his friend answered. "I don't like it."

Son trotted forward and positioned his horse between

the two northerners. Peering down the long stretch, he could see a carriage partially blocking the road, and a man sitting on a horse. There were also other men leaning against the hedge walls along the road. Though he couldn't tell what was happening from such a distance, he didn't feel good about it.

"A blockade," Brunnlyn said in a low voice, and he brought his horse to an even slower stride.

The other two did the same, keeping their horses evenly positioned across the road.

Son had never seen a blockade before, and wondered why one would be situated so far outside any village or city. "What are we going to do?"

Dulnear's eyes formed narrow slits as he peered ahead. Scratching his cheek in thought he said, "I do not know if they are watching us. If we try to go around, they may pursue. If we go back to find another route, it will mean more delays in reaching Faymia. We will go through, and hope for the best."

Brunnlyn exhaled a low chuckle. Keeping watch ahead, he grunted, "Hope. The worst kind of strategy."

"Tis true," Dulnear answered. "Hope wins no battles. But it is far better than despair."

"Agreed," his companion said, raising his eyebrows in consideration.

"Maybe when they see that we have two northerners, they'll just wave us through," Son chimed in. He was hoping his companions projected enough intimidation to avoid confrontation.

As they rode closer to the roadblock, Dulnear's jaw clenched as his eyes narrowed further and his lip curled upward. "Now I see," he began. "They are slavers. I can smell their horrible cologne from here."

When Son heard the words, his spine stiffened and his mind raced. After his encounter in Dorcadas, he never wanted to see another slaver again. "Are you sure it's not too late to turn back?" he asked. "I mean, that is a viable option."

As if to answer the boy's question, the slaver sitting atop his horse called out, "You there! Keep moving forward!"

Keeping his face forward, Dulnear said quietly, "Do not increase your pace. These men have no authority."

Brunnlyn could be heard taking loud, deep breaths and counting quietly. "I count only six," he announced. "If we are delayed, it shall not be for long."

"Agreed," Dulnear concurred. "However, we shall do our best to pass peacefully."

"Halt," the man upon the horse said. He was dark, and whiskery, and his fine clothes looked as if they had seen better days. As he examined the three travelers, his eyes suddenly became wider and he glanced nervously back at his companions.

"Why are you stopping us?" Dulnear asked. His voice was deep and slow, and his eyes moved back and forth from the man on the horse to his lackeys along the road.

The man cleared his throat. His fingers twitched and the corner of his mouth crept upward. "We are looking for someone," he said.

"Well, it looks like you have found three someones," Dulnear replied. "Now, may we please pass by?"

"I'm afraid I can't let you do that," the man asserted.

"My name is Trossed, and my client has paid me a large sum of money to set up blockades in order to find a certain person."

"Blockades?" Dulnear questioned. "You mean this is not the only one?"

"That's right," the man informed. "We figured we'd find you closer to Laor, but it was my idea to look further out."

When Son heard the man's words, he felt his stomach turn. The whole world around him seemed to wave like the sea, and he looked intently at his friend.

With characteristic calmness, Dulnear replied, "If you went through all this trouble so you can congratulate me on being a great man, then I accept. Now, please get out of our way."

At that, Brunnlyn burst out with laughter. Looking at his fellow northerner he said, "You really do know how to find trouble, my friend. You have a gift."

"I disagree," Dulnear replied. "I believe it is trouble that is very good at finding me." Turning his attention toward Trossed, he asked, "What does a slaver want with me?"

The man goaded his horse a step toward the travelers. His eyelids came closer together and his lip stiffened. "I'm a bounty hunter, not a slaver," he began. "But my client is a slaver. I am on business from Ocmallum, and the boy you're riding with is coming with me."

⋙————•————

Dulnear felt his spine fill with iron. He was fiercely committed to protecting Son, and he yearned to be with

Faymia without delay. Dispensing with pleasantries, he threatened, "You will let us pass, or we will lay waste to your little blockade."

A crooked smile found its way across Trossed the bounty hunter's face. He led his horse toward the carriage and hissed, "You northerners think you're so mighty. Well, today you're going to do as you're told, or your oversized egos will litter the side of the road." He then tapped the side of the wagon and its door flew open.

Dulnear pulled his horse back a couple steps and watched heavily armed men begin to pile out of the carriage. With armor that was painted black, and weapons that appeared well worn, they filed in front of the bounty hunter and formed a line across the road. Once they were in their place, the men who were leaning against the hedges joined them from behind, forming a second line.

Brunnlyn withdrew his sword and leaned across Son toward his fellow northerner. He pursed his lips in a disappointed frown. "Looks like I miscounted," he mumbled.

"Your brute squad does not frighten us," Dulnear growled. "This is your last warning. Let us pass, or bleed out. The choice is yours."

The bounty hunter chuckled. Cocking his head sideways, he boomed, "Do you know who these men are? They are Greyus warriors, and they show no mercy!"

Taking his sword from its sheath, Dulnear taunted, "I have seen more intimidating lumps in a cow pasture."

One of Trossed's eyebrows shot up in bemusement. "You really aren't afraid, are you," he observed. "Well, today—"

The bounty hunter was interrupted when Dulnear

spun his horse around, causing it to kick one of the Greyus warriors backward into another thug. The warrior lay motionless as the thug struggled to get out from underneath him. "I told you that you were out of chances!" the northerner yelled as he charged forward, bringing his sword down on another of the gang. This time his attack was blocked and the Greyus swung back, nearly catching Dulnear's hand.

"Kill the northerners, but bring the boy to me unharmed!" Trossed cried out, and the band of warriors and bounty hunter henchmen rushed out to assault the travelers.

Dulnear replayed the previous moments in his mind, second-guessing his approach to the situation. But his rumination ended quickly as he found his horse surrounded by Greyus. Feeling he could fare better without it, he swung the animal around once more and dismounted with a heavy kick to the head of one of his attackers.

"Perhaps these men have been practicing!" Brunnlyn shouted above the melee. He had also gotten down from his horse and was hacking away at Trossed's men.

Dulnear noticed that two of the bounty hunter's goons were reaching for Son. He swiped his sword upward, taking off one of the men's right arm. "Ride north till you are out of reach!" he yelled to the boy.

Son pulled the reins hard and his steed bucked and turned around. He then gave it a firm kick, causing it to bolt northward.

Immediately, Trossed rushed through the crowd to chase after Son, but not before Dulnear caught him with the tip of his sword, sending him to the ground, and his horse off without a rider.

"You will regret that!" the bounty hunter bellowed as he bounced to his feet and withdrew his weapon.

Dulnear was surprised to see such a rapid recovery. Just then, one of the Greyus warriors thrust his sword toward the northerner. He redirected the blade with his own and sent the man stumbling toward Trossed. Trossed stepped out of the way quickly and spun with his sword extended, cutting a swath across the front of Dulnear's coat.

The man from the north showed his teeth and emitted a low growl. "This was my father's coat, you pathetic miscreant," he blasted.

"Oh?" the bounty hunter teased. He then took a knife from inside his vest and, with both of his weapons, made several more cuts into the coat before Dulnear had a chance to react.

Dulnear now knew there was more to Trossed than he had originally suspected. He took a step back, planted his left foot firmly behind him, and mentally formed a strategy for breaking the man.

>>>———·————·—

Brunnlyn moved swiftly and skillfully. Having cut through all of the bounty hunter's thugs, only the Greyus warriors remained. He would have been confident the battle would be over soon, but the warriors had shown as uncanny ability to recover from his attacks in quick fashion.

Suddenly, he found himself besieged by three warriors at once. He darted to his right, smashing the nearest attacker with his forearm while thrusting his sword into the neck of the warrior behind him. As the third advanced, he kicked and missed. The warrior took the opportunity to chop down on Brunnlyn's leg, carving a gash into his thigh.

The northerner reacted quickly, bringing his sword down on the Greyus warrior's shoulder, cleaving off his arm and sending it to the ground. As he stepped back, to his dismay, two of his opponents were on their feet advancing again, one of them showing surprising ferocity for missing a limb.

"By the sword of Konungr," he said to himself. "The time for even the slightest mercy is over."

Just then, another Greyus warrior joined the two, swinging a mace, and nearly landing a blow to Brunnlyn's temple. The northerner crouched and assessed his options. He had hoped to be done fighting when he surrendered his hand, but here he was, surrounded by fighters clad in black armor who were showing remarkable endurance.

"How do you keep getting back up?" he shouted as he swung his sword in a fast, downward arc, lopping off the leg of the man nearest to him.

Then, as the two others progressed forward, he yelled again, "How are you doing this?!"

There was no answer. Only the eerie, frantic movements of his resilient opponents.

Before Brunnlyn had a chance to put his sword through the back of his one-legged opponent, another Greyus warrior was clinging to the back of his neck, thrusting a knife into his shoulder. He released a deep growl in pain as he attempted to knock the fighter off with his right forearm.

The northerner then swung his sword in a circle while lowering his head forward. It caught the savage's head, knocking his helmet off. His skin was pale, and his mouth stained with a blackness similar to his armor. As the warrior hissed, Brunnlyn swung his sword again, this time removing a section of the Greyus's skull, dropping him to the ground, lifeless.

The northerner looked down at the corpse with disgust. When he looked back up, there were now five of the armored combatants upon him. Lurching forward, he swung his sword with the speed and precision of one trained to do so since he was a mere child. Had he his right hand, the battle might have been over by now, but the mysterious Greyus just kept coming.

>>>———•———→

"You should have just let me take the boy," Trossed blustered. "Now, you and your furry countryman will die for nothing."

Dulnear continued to size up his opponent. Not everything was as it seemed. That much was clear to him. "Why does Ocmallum want him?" he asked. "And why not me? I was there in his chamber. I fought his elite guard."

"I don't care," the bounty hunter spat. "I am simply paid to do a job, and I always deliver."

"Well, I hate to ruin your perfect record," the man from the north huffed. He then swung his sword inward toward the man's neck.

Surprisingly, Trossed arched backward while raising his

sword to block the attack. His defense happened so quickly, it almost appeared as if it was choreographed in advance.

Taken aback—but not for long—Dulnear came at the man again, but each swipe of his blade was either dodged or blocked until, finally, he landed a steel-fisted punch to the man's face, shattering his nose and sending him flying backward.

As if the blow never landed, Trossed returned to his position with expediency. Wiping the blood from his face, he threatened, "That's a neat toy you have there. I will take it off your dead body as a souvenir." He then returned Dulnear's attack, swiping with his knife in one hand and sword in the other.

The man from the north managed to block most of the bounty hunter's strikes, but a stab to the ribs landed, almost puncturing his lung. Growing more uncertain about this man, and more impatient with each passing second, he managed to land a punch to his abdomen, then brought his sword down and around, removing two of Trossed's fingers on his right hand.

The bounty hunter neither cried in pain nor dropped his sword; instead, he kept fighting. As Dulnear exchanged blows with him, he noticed that all of the remaining Greyus warriors were now attacking Brunnlyn, and his friend was tiring. He kicked Trossed back, then slashed to the right. Knowing he would block, he aimed lower, taking off the man's right hand.

Trossed watched his hand and sword drop to the ground. "I was fond of that hand," he said morbidly. Then, like lightning, he slid behind Dulnear and begun stabbing him in the back.

The man from the north tried turning but each time, the bounty hunter maneuvered behind him.

Dulnear knew he couldn't endure the punishment for long. He gave a violent spin, hoping to take off Trossed's head, but only hit him with the pommel of his sword, knocking him a long step backward.

The bounty hunter growled, becoming more animal-like. He bore a set of stained teeth and started to advance when a distant shout distracted him. He looked over his shoulder to see Son racing toward them at full speed. "So, the boy thinks he can save you. How cute," he rasped.

"Run!" Son yelled. "Move!"

Dulnear used the distraction to attack Trossed once more. Once again, his sword was dodged and the man was suddenly standing toe to toe with him, holding his knife to the northerner's throat. However, before he had a chance to cut him, Son rode right by without slowing down.

"Run!" the boy cried out again.

Licking his lips, Trossed taunted, "It matters not where the boy goes. We will find him, and we will—" Trossed was abruptly and violently pulled back. Like a toy, he was being tossed about by the enormous, bloodthirsty kottur.

Dulnear was shocked by what he was seeing. The mountain creature had tracked them all the way from Tuas-Arum, and was now tearing his opponent apart. The animal tore a mouthful from the bounty hunter's neck, leaving his head barely attached. It then released a roar that would have paralyzed the stoutest of men with fear.

Brunnlyn rolled away from the mob of warriors, putting them between himself and the kottur. The beast then dove into the gang of Greyus fighters and began shredding them with razor claws and fangs.

"Let's go!" Son shouted from his horse. He had already gathered the reins of the other two horses and was waiting near the carriage.

Dulnear watched as the great cat clawed and tore at the armor-clad thugs. He felt a guilty sense of satisfaction to see their blood spilled on the road. When he realized the Greyus may be more than she could handle, he shouted to his friend, "Let us join her!"

Brunnlyn appeared puzzled, then shrugged his shoulders and began to hack away at the warriors. Dulnear led the charge, and soon there was only a vicious kottur smelling the slain henchmen and occasionally pulling off a piece of exposed flesh.

"That is disgusting," Dulnear grimaced. He sheathed his sword, stepped closer to the monster and asked, "Did you follow us all the way from the Petraig?" He then scratched its back and smiled.

The animal sniffed the man from the north and gave his beard a slobbering, bloody lick.

"I think you have a pet," Brunnlyn observed.

"No, she is just a lost soul," Dulnear replied.

"Did you not feed her?" his countryman asked.

"I did."

"Then you have a pet," Brunnlyn chuckled.

Dulnear motioned for Son to come to him. "You led her right to us," he said. "Come and let her get to know you."

The boy shook his head no. He then backed his horse up a little further while rubbing the place on his shoulder the animal had managed to get its teeth into. "I'm still sore from the first time we met," he protested. "Almost ate me whole."

The man from the north shook his head and grinned. "It will be fine. I promise, she will not hurt you."

Son reluctantly dismounted his horse and approached. As he did, he held his knife in his right hand, hoping it would do him some good if the animal turned on him.

As the three stood together, the beast nuzzled against Dulnear's chest, almost knocking him over. Scratching behind its ears he declared, "I shall name her Verrox." He then gave its neck a firm pat and asked, "Is that all right with you, large one?"

As if the animal understood, she gave the man's beard another sloppy lick.

Dulnear then directed the animal's attention toward the boy. "This is my good friend, Son," he said. "Please do not try to eat him again."

Verrox moved closer to Son, swiped its bloody snout across the boy's face, then licked it.

"Yuck!" Son croaked. "It smells like a dead man ate a dirty diaper!"

Dulnear sighed, "Ah, do not berate her. She just helped us." He then led the beastly cat toward Brunnlyn and introduced him. "This is Brunnlyn. He is my friend as well. He is grateful for your assistance."

Brunnlyn reached over and stroked the top of the animal's head. As he did, it gave him a rough, wet lick across the face. "Very nice to have you," he said to the beast. He then looked at Dulnear and repeatedly waved his hand in front of his face. "That odor really is bad," he whispered.

Dulnear rubbed his chin as he surveyed the bodies strewn across the road. He knew he had to reach Faymia, but there was a mystery that needed solving. Using his foot, he turned the mangled bounty hunter's body over and examined the dark, stained teeth protruding from its open mouth.

"The Greyus' teeth looked the same," Brunnlyn observed as he joined Dulnear. "Dark and disgusting."

Son soon joined them, and he wrinkled his nose in revulsion at the sight of Trossed's corpse. "I thought you would have made quick work of these men," he said. "What happened?"

Brunnlyn shook his head as he scratched it. "They were like rabid animals. They refused to stop attacking until they were dead. It was as if they felt no pain, regardless of the wound. I have never seen anything like it."

"I have," Dulnear breathed in a low voice. "Ocmallum's guards were the same way. The difference was, they were trained to fight in total darkness. Their eyes were even sewn shut."

"How were they able to keep fighting?" the boy asked.

Dulnear looked around, then up toward the gloomy sky. "I do not know," he answered. "But we may find some clues in that carriage." He then walked over to the darkly painted coach and cautiously opened the door. The stench from inside almost caused him to gag. There were pieces of armor lying about and a few shoddy-looking weapons. Perched on one of the seats was a large wooden bowl that caught his eye. Taking it out of the carriage, he noticed it was nearly empty, with the exception of a handful of dark-purple berries. They were oddly shaped, with larger-than-normal, bulbous drupelets.

"Have you ever seen these?" he asked his companions.

"Once. Possibly," Brunnlyn answered. "They look like the borb. But I thought they only grew on the far-southern island of Vahsi."

The man from the north held a berry between his thumb and forefinger, examining it intently. "I would say the color matches quite closely with the teeth of these fighters," he observed. He then smelled it and was taken aback. The effect was much like that of getting water up one's nose and he sneezed violently.

"What does it smell like?" Son asked.

"Like nothing I have smelled before," Dulnear replied. "Odd, like a fire radish, but putrid."

"Do you think it is what made these fighters so unrelenting?" Brunnlyn asked.

Dulnear turned the berry over, trying to make sense of its curious shape and odor. "There is only one way to find out," he said, and he placed it in his mouth, chewing it slowly. Its taste was much like its unpleasant smell. As the bitter, rotten flavor reached his throat, his eyes took in the world around him with incredible contrast and focus. He looked at his friends and noticed details about their faces he had never noticed before. He looked down at his iron hand and could see each strike the hammer left behind with perfect clarity.

"Are you unwell?" Son asked. "You seem a little..."

The boy's voice seemed louder and more defined than usual, and it agitated the man from the north. The fatigue from fighting was suddenly gone, and he had an inclination to reach for his sword. "I would say that these berries are definitely the source of their aggressiveness," he answered. Then, he paused for a moment and turned his mouth to one side in thought. "Boy, hit me," he said.

"What?" Son blurted.

Dulnear pressed his teeth together and said again, "Hit me. Go ahead and punch me right in the mouth, as hard as you can."

"Um, are you sure?" Son asked as his voice cracked.

"Definitely," the man from the north assured. "Please do it now before the effects of the berry wear off." He then got down on one knee so the boy could reach him easily. Pointing toward his own chin, he chimed, "Do it."

Son faced his mentor with great uncertainty in his eyes. He made a fist and drew back his arm.

"As hard as you can," Dulnear reminded him.

"Right, here goes," the boy announced, and he hit the man just beneath his left eye.

Dulnear stayed kneeling for a moment, rubbing his cheek. He fought back a sudden urge to retaliate. Standing to his feet, he mused, "Fascinating. I felt nothing."

"Are you sure you're not hurt?" Son asked.

"No, I am not sure," the man answered. "But your punch was nothing more than a light touch to me. It is no wonder the Greyus were not swayed by their injuries."

"Would you like me to punch you this time?" Brunnlyn asked eagerly. "It may bear more weight than the boy's."

"I would not," Dulnear answered. "It is like the pain from a blow is replaced with a violent urge to strike back. I do not know if I could subdue that urge if you were to hit me."

"I understand."

Dulnear was uncomfortable with the effect of the fruit. He inhaled as deeply as he could through his nose, then exhaled slowly through his mouth. He continued this until the world around him began to return to normal. "Besides, I would not want you to take my head off," he added with a wink. He then emptied the bowl onto the ground and stomped on the berries.

"Now we know their secret," Son confirmed. "That information may prove valuable in the future."

"Indeed it will," Dulnear agreed. "But for now, we must reach the Ohdium Rift without further delay."

"And what about the kottur?" Brunnlyn asked, gesturing toward the feasting animal.

Dulnear looked over at the beast as it lay in the road with a warrior's carcass. Walking over, he scratched behind her ear and said, "Verrox, my friend. We have to leave this place."

The animal looked at the man from the north and released a low, pleasant purr. It then yawned, baring its enormous teeth.

"It is not good for you to lay here in the road," he continued. "If you are found with these bodies, you will be hunted for sure."

Dulnear had no idea how much the beast understood, and knew he had no control over the actions of the monster. He glanced back at his friends and instructed, "Let us get these bodies off the road."

The two northerners tossed the bodies over the hedge as if they were dolls. Meanwhile, Son dragged one to the edge of the road and did his best to hide it.

"And what about that one?" Brunnlyn asked, gesturing toward the corpse the animal was still nibbling on.

"Good luck getting it from her," Dulnear replied. "I am hoping she will get out of the road sooner instead of later."

Brunnlyn chortled. With a teasing grin, he said, "The great Dulnear concerned about a foul-smelling kottur. You really have changed."

Suppressing a smile, Dulnear returned to the great cat. Leveling his eyes with hers, he spoke. "We need to be moving on. Follow us, or return to the mountains, but do not stay here long. Thank you for saving us from these savages."

Verrox lifted her tail and let it drop to the ground with a thud. She then sat up on her haunches and swiped her snout across the man's head, leaving behind more of her unpleasant odor.

As the three travelers mounted their horses and pointed them south, Dulnear looked back to see the animal still seated in the road, watching them. He whispered a brief prayer for her and rode on, setting his intention on finding Faymia as soon as he could.

## CHAPTER THIRTEEN
# RISK OR REWARD

"This is madness!" Faymia exclaimed as she and Maren worked their way down the wooden walkway that led to the neutral zone. Villagers were standing along the path's edge shouting down at the opposing army gathering below. It wasn't difficult to get by since the entire cliffside seemed to be engrossed by the growing ruckus in the Neodrec.

Stopping to catch her bearings, she recognized the empty dwelling in front of her as the place where she had met the old, blind woman. The words the stranger spoke to her echoed in her heart. "Beauty and power," she said to herself. "Harmonious music."

Breaking through the shouting crowds and the Faymia's rumination, Maren's voice could be heard asking, "How are we going to get home?"

Faymia thought hard about the past few days. She knelt on one knee and came eye to eye with the young girl. Her surroundings started to blur as she examined Maren's wild, dark hair and fair features. She gently adjust the eye patch the girl was wearing, and the weighty realization that she wanted to be just like her brought on an enormous sense of responsibility.

"You said we have to talk to the chiefs," she began. "You were right. If we have it in our power to prevent bloodshed, then we must make the attempt, even if it's not easy."

Maren nodded. Her face looked frightened, but a cast of dignity began to grow. "Uh-huh," she said. "Let's do it."

"Then we have to find a way across this mess and reach the lowground chief," Faymia exclaimed. "We have to try!"

The young girl looked intently into her face and swallowed. "All right," she whispered.

Faymia pulled the hood of her cloak forward and stood to her feet. Looking further down the walkway, she noticed that the stairway down to the next level was congested with shouting villagers. She reached for Maren and instructed, "Hold my hand, and do not let go. Do you understand?"

"Yes," the young girl said, and squeezed her hand firmly.

Keeping her back close to the cliffside dwellings, Faymia made her way past angry bands of people that scarcely resembled the inhabitants she saw just a few days before. Approaching the mob pressed together at the stairs, she lowered her head and left shoulder to push her way through, concentrating on the small hand clutched to hers. When it felt as if the movement of the crowd was going to pull her away from Maren, she moved the girl in front of herself, keeping one arm across her little friend's shoulders.

*One step*, she thought to herself as she moved her foot downward. The movements of the crowd were constant, and she feared she might find herself falling to the next platform on account of another's carelessness. She paused for a moment and looked across the tops of the heads of those on the staircase with her. To her surprise, a woman a few steps down was staring intently at her. She lowered her head and looked away from the woman, hoping she was looking at something else above her. She then moved her other foot downward while guiding Maren to do the same. *Two steps.*

"Hey!" a shrill voice yelled out. The staring woman a few steps down was now pointing directly at Faymia. "That's the traitor!" she shrieked.

>>>———•————

Faymia felt her knees become weak and her mind raced for something to say. She held Maren closely and struggled to will her legs to step back onto the walkway.

Soon, another villager turned to glare at her, and another. "What's she doing here?" a man holding a piece of black rock asked.

"I have permission to leave," Faymia finally announced, and began to retrieve the chief's letter from her tunic.

"She's a liar!" someone shouted from the staircase.

Still fumbling for the note of safe passage, Faymia felt the jagged rock strike her cheek. Instinctively, she placed her hand on her face and looked up. The man who was holding the black stone was pointing and laughing while others slowly moved up the stairs toward her. "We have to get out of here!" she yelled down at her friend.

Looking down, she noticed that Maren was now holding the stolen blackjack with one hand, slapping it against her opposite palm in a menacing fashion.

"This is not good. What are you doing?" Faymia blurted.

"People should not throw rocks!" Maren shouted, and she aimed the tip of her club toward the man who threw it.

"Bad idea!" Faymia announced. She lifted Maren up by her waist, pivoted back up onto the walkway, and began to run.

Soon, the entire mob from the stairs was on the path pursuing her. Faymia desperately tried to keep Maren's attention forward and her little feet running. The man who threw the rock caught up with them and grabbed the back of Faymia's cloak, jerking her backwards, almost pulling her off her feet.

Faymia quickly caught her bearing and spun to land a tight-fisted punch to the man's throat. He instantly grabbed at his windpipe, trying to catch his breath. The woman who first spotted Faymia and turned the crowd against her ran to assist the now-choking man.

"See! She tried to kill him!" the abrasive woman shouted. "Don't let her get away!"

As fast as she could, Faymia drew her bow and pulled back an arrow. As she did, the crowd took a step back. "I can hit a falcon atop the highest tree!" she shouted. "Now, let me go in peace or I will release this into your filthy neck!"

Glancing down, she could see Maren making threatening gestures toward the mob again. She knew aiming her weapon at a gang of whipped-up villagers wasn't the best idea she'd ever had. But the intense fear, mixed with the anger that was burning inside of her, had her thinking this may be her last stand.

Suddenly, another jagged black stone went whizzing through the air and brushed her hood as it flew past. Amidst the crowd, a portly, dark man was standing with an armful of stones, tossing them at her. Faymia released her arrow, causing it to pierce the man's hand before he had a chance to throw another.

"Yeargh!" the man cried out, dropping his rocks.

The crowd gasped, stepping away from the man.

Faymia loaded another arrow and began to take steps backward, placing herself between Maren and the group.

Soon, those who were standing around the portly man began to pick up the stones he had dropped and slowly move up the walkway. A woman flung one at Faymia, and it was returned with an arrow lodged into her shoulder.

Letting out a screech of pain, the woman wailed, "How could you?!" as she clutched her injury.

Speedily, another jagged rock flew through the air, this one striking the side of Faymia's head. She clenched her teeth and squinted, identifying the man who threw it and putting an arrow into the middle of his arm.

*They have lost their sanity*, Faymia thought to herself before a rock struck her in the shoulder. Before she had a chance to react, another one landed, and another. She fired off two more arrows, then reached into her quiver, only to discover it was now empty.

Two men at the front of the mob made their way closer. Faymia shouldered her bow and withdrew her sword. The men stepped back for a moment, then advanced again, to her left and to her right.

Swinging in a large arc to the left, Faymia cut deep into the side of the man's knee, bringing him tumbling to the walkway. The man to her right lurched at her with a shout. She swung hard right, slashing across his ribs.

The frenzied crowd seemed to be growing more aggressive by the moment and accelerated their advance. Faymia reached for Maren behind her and shouted, "Run!" and they resumed their escape.

Faymia knew running up the walkway was futile, since it only led back to the chief's quarters. However, no other options were presenting themselves. As she ran, she worried deeply about what might become of Maren if they were caught. She thought about turning around and surrendering under the condition of the girl's freedom. Just as she began to sheath her sword, she looked up ahead and to her right and saw the empty dwelling where she had met the blind woman.

For reasons unknown to Faymia, she ran as fast as she could to the dwelling, almost lifting Maren off the ground to rush her forward. She ducked inside the doorless entry and said a prayer.

Just as the enraged mob was upon the threshold, a voice cried out, "Stop!"

Faymia's heart pounded and she held tightly to Maren as she peered through the doorway from the back wall of the dwelling. She could see that those closest to the entry had halted, but were still being jostled forward by the rear of the rowdy mob. People began shouting expletives and accusations, and it wasn't long before their rumbling voices turned into a roar.

"I said stop!!" the voice called out again. This time it rang deeper, and clearer, and Faymia felt a shiver in her back as it reverberated against the walls of her shelter.

Suddenly, she saw the man behind the voice. It was Argach, the chief's assistant. He stepped into view with his sword drawn. The crowd moved back as he did. He then stepped backward through the entrance and called out, "Faymia?"

The woman was unsure whether the man was there to arrest her or to help her. She remained against the back wall of the room, covered in darkness. "Yes?" she replied tentatively.

The man turned and stepped toward her. In a low voice, he explained, "I believe you were telling the truth. Come with me, and I can get you as far as the Neodrec."

Faymia felt herself exhale in relief. Slowly stepping forward, she asked, "How are you going to get me past that herd of rock-throwing sheep?"

"Don't worry about that," Argach replied. "Do you still have the letter from Thuaid?"

Faymia reached into her tunic and withdrew the parchment. Showing it to the man, she groaned, "A lot of good this did me."

"Let me have it," the chief's assistant instructed. "Disobeying me means risking arrest and imprisonment."

Faymia handed the letter to Argach, praying this was not some form of trickery. She then followed him out through the doorway and the crowd began to grumble and hurl threats once more.

"Listen!" the man bellowed to the mob as he held up the parchment. "This is an official letter from Chief Thuaid! It declares that this woman and her companion are to receive safe passage out of the Ruhbrem territory. If any of you attempts to hinder her, by any means, you will be arrested and locked in the dungeon. If you resist arrest, I will run you through, be you man, woman, or child. Do I make myself clear?"

The grumbling immediately died down and several villagers dropped their stones to the ground. Creating a path down the walkway, they stepped toward either side of it to let Argach, Faymia, and Maren through.

>>> ———— ·———— ——

Faymia kept her hood up and her head low as Argach guided her down the wooden path. After sheathing his sword, the chief's assistant kept his left arm around her shoulder, and held Maren's hand with his right, as he lead them.

Once they were past the rowdy, rock-throwing crowd and down the next flight of stairs, they hardly seemed to be noticed. From time to time, someone would lock eyes with Faymia and scowl, but then they would turn away. She thought perhaps those villagers assumed she was under Argach's custody and was being moved to another dungeon or escorted out of the Rift. Either way, she was happy not to have a gang of rabble chasing her up a cliffside.

The further they moved toward the last leg of the walkway, the thicker the crowds became. From time to time, the chief's assistant would shout at or nudge a villager to get them to clear a path.

Faymia observed that there seemed to be a mania overtaking those closer to the bottom of the Ohdium. Their faces were twisted and crimson, and they shouted things filled with vitriol but void of logic. She glanced out into the neutral zone and could see troops from both sides snarling at each other like animals. There was soon to be much bloodshed, and it was all on account of greedy men who valued attention and silver more than truth and peace.

Finally, they reached the place where the walkway spilled out into the Neodrec. Above the noise all around them, Argach shouted to Faymia and Maren, "I can only take you a little further! If I'm seen beyond the center line, I'm as good as dead!"

The woman nodded in acknowledgement and looked around to study her surroundings.

When they were on the fringe of the mass of soldiers, the chief's assistant took Maren's hand and joined it with Faymia's. He crouched down and wrapped his arms around the girl, then stood to face her guardian. "I will return immediately to Thuaid and try once more to persuade him to call off this madness," he said. "I'm sorry your holiday turned out so disastrous."

"Thank you for your help," Faymia said. "I think we'll just visit the sea next time."

Argach smiled at the woman's statement and added, "Then you'd better leave now or there may not be a next time."

Faymia and Maren turned north and began making their way toward the narrow part of the ravine where their horse was waiting. As the sound of the roaring mob faded behind them, they stopped. "Well, my friend," the woman began. "We made it halfway. Do you still believe we should try to reach the lowground chief?"

Maren sighed, then muttered, "Uh-huh."

Faymia looked around the neutral territory once more

and took a deep breath. "At least we won't be trapped against a cliff," she said. "We can travel through the woods, and you can show me how to reach the village."

Maren squeezed her hand a little tighter and began walking toward the tree line. As they walked, she said, "I have a question."

"Yes?"

"Can we really go to the sea?"

Faymia couldn't help but giggle at the timing of the question. "Of course," she answered.

CHAPTER FOURTEEN

# THE TAALBREM

"How much further?" Faymia asked. The reality of spending the night on a dungeon floor was catching up with her tired body. Her neck ached, and the pain was creeping up toward the base of her skull.

"Just a little more and we'll be at the edge of the village," Maren answered.

They had traveled through the woods that grew along the western edge of the neutral zone and emerged out into the fields that lay beyond it. Once they were in the open, they carefully walked north as the land rolled upward toward the Taalbrem hamlet.

When they arrived at the town's edge, Faymia noticed how deserted it seemed. It was a far cry from the chaos of the Ruhbrem's cliffside settlement. She could hear the breeze blowing across the tall grass behind them, and wanted to drink in the stillness for a moment before going any further.

"There," Maren said, breaking the silence. She was

pointing far off, toward the largest and most ornate structure in the village. She continued, "That is where Le'as lives. He's a nice man, but he thinks I'm like William, the boy without any legs. I have two perfectly good ones."

Faymia looked down at her friend and tilted her head sideways. Her curiosity was piqued, but she didn't have time to unravel what she had just said. "Well, let's hope he's home," she answered.

As they entered the town's center and began to approach the Reonem, Maren chirped, "This is the table where the chiefs would meet and reason together."

Faymia was caught off guard by the beauty of the setting. She marveled at the intricate carvings on the stone table that sat around the tree and slowly ran her hand across its surface.

Suddenly, a voice broke through the air. "What are you doing here?!"

Faymia looked to see a muscular woman standing between two men that appeared to be guards. Her arms were bare, and her hair was pulled back into a braid so tight her eyes took on a slanted quality.

"That's Soeth, the chief's guard," Maren whispered. She nervously massaged her ear and inched herself closer to Faymia's side.

"Well, it would have been nice to know about her before we arrived," Faymia sighed in return. "Here we go again."

"Say, I know you. You're that little girl I plucked out of the woods," Soeth said. "Where did you go the other day?"

Maren squeezed her ear and stared up at the woman. Finally, she answered, "I went to get my friend. This is Faymia."

Faymia nodded. She wanted to hope that the people of the lowground were more reasonable than those she experienced amongst the cliff dwellings, but was afraid it was only a fool's hope. "Pleased to meet you," she spoke politely as she nodded toward the woman.

Soeth quickly glanced at Faymia from head to toe, then met Maren's eyes. "I'm afraid you returned at a bad time," she said. "Most of the village is at the Neodrec, preparing to take the cliffs before those filthy Ruhbrem have a chance to attack us on Taalbrem ground."

"That is why we must see your chief," Faymia broke in. "What is about to happen is avoidable. We just need to talk with him."

Though it didn't seem possible, Soeth's face took on an even harder, more stone-like demeanor. She shot a knowing glance to the guards on either side of her and her shoulders broadened. "What did you just say?"

"We must speak with your chief," Faymia began. "There are forces at play that have been pitting the people of the Ohdium against each other."

Soeth clenched her jaw and curled her upper lip. "That is not going to happen!" she barked. "Leave now, or—"

"You'll arrest me as an instigator?" Faymia interrupted. She was tired and frustrated, and didn't understand why she couldn't just walk away from these angry, petty, self-destructive people. After the way they judged each other, spitefully spoke out of ignorance and pride, and refused to listen, perhaps they deserved the pain and bloodshed of war. But that would deny the world of the beauty they could once again display together. Their power would be great, and their song ever so lovely. "I've already been arrested, thrown into a dungeon, and attacked by a mob. Nothing is going to keep me from seeing your chief!" Faymia proclaimed. Her fists curled into tight balls and she raised her chin. She could see no other chance of stopping the war if she failed here. "Now, let us through!" she demanded.

Soeth stood unmoved. She pulled a well-polished sword from its sheath and announced, "No!" As she did, the guards on either side of her did the same.

Faymia took a breath so deep her shoulders and chest expanded to an unnatural degree. It felt to her as if her entire body had become more awake than she had ever experienced before. She withdrew her sword and planted her right foot behind her. She glanced at Maren and murmured a few words in northern-speak that she had learned from her husband, hoping the young girl knew what she was saying. Maren nodded in return and took a small step backward.

For a moment, the five adversaries stood there, meeting each other's eyes. The quiet of the village was replaced by a droning pulse in Faymia's ears. She could feel a drop of sweat run down her side as her mind rehearsed her next few movements.

Suddenly, Soeth let loose a deafening scream and lurched forward, bringing her sword down with a swoosh that cut through the air.

In a single motion, Faymia stepped to her left, pulled the stolen blackjack from her tunic, and smashed it with all of her strength against the ear of the nearest guard. Before his hand could instinctively reach up to touch the throbbing wound, he was stumbling around like a drunken sailor, eventually falling face-first to the ground.

Soeth stepped over the man and growled, "You're going to pay for that, outsider!"

Faymia stood powerfully, facing the woman. She held her sword in her right hand at the ready. With her left hand, she held the baton against her forearm. Her eye focused on the eyes of her opponent and she bared her teeth. Speaking in a low, confident tone, she breathed, "Come and get me."

>>>⸺•⸺

"Get over here!" one of the guards yelled, dashing toward Maren.

The girl ducked out of the way and stepped to the right, causing the man to stumble forward. As she did, she withdrew her blackjack and cocked her arm back, ready to strike.

The guard regained his footing and faced Maren once more. "Do you seriously think you're going to hurt me with that?" he asked with an amused grin.

"Knee!" Maren shouted, and sprinted past the man while smacking the side of his right knee.

"Hey!" the guard moaned as he nearly buckled to the ground. Withdrawing his sword, he pointed its tip toward her and blurted, "You won't do that again!"

Maren ran toward the man, attempting to wound his other knee. When she did, the man lowered his sword, deflecting the club. He then quickly landed the back of his fist against the back of her head, sending her reeling forward a few steps before falling to her hands and knees.

Maren shook the sudden disequilibrium from her head, rolled on the ground to her right, and sprang to her feet. She was soon facing the man with her weapon ready to strike once again.

Spinning around to face the girl, the guard lunged forward with his blade, narrowly missing her neck. Clearly frustrated that defeating a child was proving to be more difficult than it should be, he growled and raised his sword above his head.

As the guard's sword was still held aloft, Maren struck his shin with the baton. The sudden injury caused him to reflexively bend over, and she caught the side of his head with the blunt weapon.

The man bellowed like a teakettle as he shot up straight. Before Maren had a chance to strike again, he kicked her hard in the stomach, sending her flying backward, then landing on her face.

Maren felt as if all the air in the world was gone and she struggled to take a breath. She hefted herself up onto her hands and feet, knowing it would only be moments before the man struck her again, this time with his sword.

Digging deep within, she crawled backward. As she did, she noticed that her left hand was on a stone the size of her fist, and her right hand was still clutching the blackjack. She sprang to her feet and threw the rock at the charging guard's waist. He lowered both arms to block it and, as he did, she threw her club as hard as she could at the man's face, squarely thumping his nose, causing his nostrils to stream blood to the ground like neither of them had seen before.

"You broke my nose!" the man cried as he wiped the blood from his upper lip with his free hand.

As the man was bewailing his newest injury, Maren darted toward him, retrieved the blackjack, and positioned herself behind him.

Before he could turn around, the girl scaled his back like a frightened feline. She then hooked her legs over his shoulders and began hammering the top of his head with her weapon. In an attempt to shake the girl lose, he jerked his body quickly, but the motion only served to aggravate the damage she had done to his knee and it gave out, causing him to drop to both knees.

Maren leaped forward from the man's shoulders, landing on both feet. Like a top, she spun around, raised her blackjack, and bashed the side of his head, holding nothing back.

For a brief moment the guard shifted one leg forward, as if trying to return to his feet. He then opened his mouth and closed it again. Maren thought he was trying to say something and assumed the knock on his head caused him to immediately forget it. He then let out a sigh as his damaged leg gave out and he fell to his bottom. Shortly after, his entire body fell sideways and he lay down in the dirt.

"I don't like outsiders, I don't like your little brat, and I don't like you!" Soeth scathed. She advanced toward Faymia, leading with a long, broad double-edged sword.

Faymia's muscles tensed and she grasped her weapons with a steel grip. She held the guard's eyes in her gaze, watching for the slightest hint of her charging. Her grace for these people had been spent. She could not understand their reasoning, nor their insistence on ignoring her warnings. It was beyond her comprehension. Angrily, she snarled, "You deserve the fate coming to you if you try to stop me!"

"Oh, you mean the war?" Soeth taunted. She then chortled, "I'll be safely off with Gadoar and Breag, dividing our bounty as we drink to a successful campaign."

Faymia couldn't believe what she was hearing. Before her mouth could form the words that were spinning through her head, her right hand was slashing her sword inward, just missing the broad woman's fingers.

Soeth growled and countered the attack by lunging her sword forward. As she did, Faymia stepped right and hooked her left fist in so the baton she was holding struck the woman in the mouth.

The chief's guard bared her teeth and spit blood before backhanding Faymia on the temple.

Faymia stumbled to her right, willing her body to stay ready to fight. Soeth was much stronger than she had anticipated. She lunged forward with her sword, aiming for Soeth's neck, but the guard pivoted left, blocking Faymia and nearly disarming her.

Soeth then returned her sword right, bringing its tip across Faymia's collar, slicing through fabric and skin.

Faymia suppressed the urge to shout in pain and resumed her attack. "I knew those two good-for-nothings weren't acting alone," she said as she swung waist-level.

Soeth parried Faymia's attack while stepping forward with a swift left hook.

Stepping backward and trying to shake the blow to her cheek before the guard attacked again, Faymia continued. "You must be pretty lonely to be making time with those wastrels." She then released an exhausted chuckle and resumed her fighting stance, keeping the blackjack firmly pressed against her left forearm and her right hand ready to deliver a sword strike.

Clearly offended by the remark, Soeth slashed wildly without much apparent thought. Though Faymia was able to block each swing, the guard's strength made it difficult to stay upright.

As they sparred, it occurred to Faymia how easily angered and offended Soeth was, so she used it to her advantage. "What's the matter?" she asked. "Is it hard to get any other men to spend time with you?"

"What?!" the guard screeched. "You're going to pay for that!"

"Well, I might need to borrow some of your thornback blood money to do so," Faymia taunted.

Again Soeth aggressed with a snarl, slicing the air downward over and over. Each time, Faymia blocked with the club in her left hand. Her arm grew more fatigued with each blow until, suddenly, she stepped backward, causing the woman to slightly lose her forward balance.

Faymia took the opportunity to bring her own sword down now. With a whoosh, she chopped the other woman's right shoulder, causing her to wobble forward, dropping her sword as she cried out in pain.

Using her own momentum, Soeth dove for Faymia's legs. She wrapped her left arm around them, taking the woman down to her back. She positioned herself above and began raining punches down on her face and neck.

Faymia knew she would not live if she stayed in this position. Her sword was useless here, and the quarters were too close to use the blackjack offensively. With a burst of speed and strength, she wiggled onto her stomach, then pushed herself up to her hands and knees.

Furiously, Soeth beat down on the back of Faymia's head with her left fist, her body draped across her back. Thinking fast, Faymia timed the hammering of the guard's arms and when she recoiled one of her arms to strike another blow, she grabbed it and held it tightly against herself. She then threw her hips as hard as she could while raising her knee sharply, sending Soeth to the ground while still maintaining control of the arm, barring it hard against her knee.

The sound of a muffled tear could be heard from the guard's arm and she howled like an injured coyote. "You broke my arm, you filthy ronyon!"

Faymia quickly rose to her feet, stood above Soeth, and brought her club down on the woman's broken elbow. As she bellowed in pain, Faymia gave a blow to her temple. "Now, I'm going to talk to your chief, whether you like it or not!" she declared, and hit her one last time.

>>> ———— • ————

Following a fleet-footed Maren, Faymia ran into the chief's chambers. Like Thuaid, he sat at a table with several parchments strewn across it. There were no guards in the room, and the man appeared dressed to go to battle.

"Mister Le'as," Maren chirped loudly. "Something terrible is happening, and I brought my friend Faymia to help."

Startled, the chief looked up from the table. Tilting his head sideways and narrowing his eyes, he exclaimed, "Maren? I'm surprised to see you here. After you disappeared, I thought I'd never see you again."

"I beg your forgiveness," Faymia broke in, stepping closer to the table. "She came to retrieve me. There is a plot brewing that will bring ruin to the entire Ohdium. We had to warn you."

Le'as stared at the woman for a moment, his blue eyes conveying speculation and disbelief. "Warn me?" he groaned. "I already know of the Ruhbrem's imminent attack, and have dispatched my men to the Neodrec to hold them back."

Faymia did not want to waste time with the chief. Replaying her conversation with Thuaid in her mind, she quickly thought of another approach. "How did you come by the news of the cliff dwellers' attack?" she asked.

"From my loyal scout Breag, of course," the man answered.

Staying calm and keeping expressions of anger at bay, Faymia continued. "And may I ask where your scout is now?"

"I sent him to the neutral zone to take note of events there. He should be reporting back to me shortly."

Faymia silently inhaled, then swallowed. Keeping a cool demeanor, she replied, "Sir, we were just in the Neodrec, and Breag was not present."

The chief's head cocked back and his forehead wrinkled. "Are you sure?"

"Yes, sir," the woman answered. Then, carefully, she attempted to tell of the orchestrated war the best she could without stoking the flames of skepticism. "I overheard him near the neutral zone the other day. He was speaking with another man about leaving the village."

"Leaving the village?!" Le'as bellowed. Standing to his feet, he demanded, "Who was this other man?"

Faymia considered her words wisely. Looking up and to the right, she pushed her mouth to the side in an effort to pretend she was trying to remember. Finally, she answered in a manner that half-sounded like a question, "I believe he called himself Gadoar."

"Gadoar?" Le'as shouted. "Why, he is a scout for the Ruhbrem! Breag has no business with that man!"

"Really?" Faymia feigned shock. "They were saying something about reporting things that were not true in order to increase their coffers. And I think I heard one of them say that instigating a war was lucrative business."

The chief looked dizzy. He grabbed ahold of the table in front of him to steady himself. "I've been betrayed," he lamented. "I don't know what to do."

"Call back your men," Faymia pleaded. "If the Ruhbrem believe they are defending themselves from an imminent attack by the Taalbrem, perhaps your action will set them at ease and they will also withdraw."

Le'as wrung his hands and began to pace back and

forth. "I cannot believe I allowed this to happen," he stammered. "I feel like a fool."

Faymia knew she stood on uncertain ground. She watched the chief walk and ponder the situation. Finally, she asked, "How can I serve you in this?"

Le'as looked at Faymia as if he wanted to say something, but the words themselves refused to come out.

Suddenly, the door flew open with a crash and there stood Soeth, followed by six well-armed soldiers. "Do not listen to her!" she cried out, and ran into the chamber to apprehend Faymia and Maren.

## CHAPTER FIFTEEN
# SCHEMES AND SCREAMS

Faymia stood frozen as Soeth and the armed soldiers filed into the room. Maren took her hand and squeezed it tightly. Thinking fast, she called out to the chief, "She's in on it! She has been conspiring with the scouts!"

Le'as looked around the room. Confusion was written all over his face. He ran out from behind his table and stood between Faymia and his head guard. "Is it true?" he questioned Soeth. "Did you help stir up this war?"

The muscular woman rolled her left hand into a fist and cleared her throat. "Absolutely not, my liege. This one-eyed harpy attacked myself and my guards, then ran in here screeching something about killing you," she sneered.

"What?! That's not true!" Faymia declared. "I came to warn you!"

Le'as watched intently as the two women volleyed their argument back and forth. As he did, the confusion on his face gave way to terrified concern and fatigue. After several minutes, he interrupted. "Enough!" Then, his features softened and he looked closely at Maren. Approaching her, he took to one knee and said, "Blessed one, when you were here last, you spoke truth, even when it made William uncomfortable."

Maren, appearing somewhat embarrassed, shrugged her shoulders and answered, "Uh-huh."

"I believe you are very skilled at telling the truth," the man continued. "Is that correct?"

"I reckon so," the girl answered, scratching the side of her head.

The chief tilted his head and rubbed his chin. "Then I'm confident I would be able to tell if you were not speaking the truth," he observed.

"It's true. She is horribly inept at telling lies," Faymia interrupted.

Le'as lifted a finger toward Faymia, gesturing that he would like her to remain silent. He then looked deeply into Maren's eyes and asked, "Is the story your friend is telling true? Did the scouts encourage this war, and is Soeth aligned with them?"

"Yes, sir," Maren answered while nodding her head up and down.

The chief took a deep breath and paused. Staring at the girl, he exhaled slowly, then leaned in and spoke quietly into her ear, "I believe you."

Le'as then stood and turned toward Soeth. Raising his voice to fill the room with the sound of his authority, he boomed, "You are a traitor to your chief, and to your people! Guards, arrest her!"

Soeth's expression turned to disgust. She glanced around the room, then met eyes with the chief. Slowly, a smirk crept across her face, as if the corners of her mouth thought for themselves. "Well, I was going to kill you after the war broke out, but I might as well do it now," she sneered. She then moved further into the room, flanked by the soldiers accompanying her.

"So, it is treason then," Le'as lamented. He then withdrew a well-polished sword from the scabbard at his waist.

Soeth cackled in amusement as she watched the chief aim his blade at her. "You might as well surrender," she said. "There are seven of us, and only three of you." She then looked down at Maren and added, "Make that two and a half."

"The little one took out one of your men," Faymia interjected. "Don't be overconfident."

"Luck!" Soeth screeched. "This is your last warning. Surrender, and we will make your death quick and painless. Resist, and we will enjoy removing your skin first."

Faymia could feel her blood boiling at the sound of the woman's voice. She knew she would not live if she surrendered and, if she was going to die today, she was determined to take Soeth with her. She withdrew her sword and stood next to Le'as. "I will fight beside the chief!" she declared.

"Me too!" called out Maren as she joined her friend. Once again, she had her blackjack in one hand as she menacingly smacked it against the other.

Soeth stepped forward, and the soldiers on either side of her pointed the tips of their swords toward the three defenders. In a mocking voice she gibed, "Sir, it has been a pleasure serving you. Consider this my resignation from your dim-witted service."

Taking another step closer, Soeth's attention was drawn to the large window behind the chief's throne. There was a boyish figure pressing his face toward the pane with his hands wrapped around his eyes. He turned his head and yelled something, then resumed gazing through the window into the chief's chamber.

"What's going on out there?" Soeth barked, but the soldiers looked just as confused as she did.

Faymia glanced over her shoulder at the window, then back at her attackers. Suppressing a smile, she said, "Looks like a village boy has stumbled onto your plot. Are you going to kill him too?"

Soeth looked around the room, then back at the window where the boy was still staring in. Now, with less confidence, she replied, "Perhaps. What's one more body to the pile when I'll soon be gone from this forsaken place?"

Faymia now smiled openly and glanced behind the guard and her soldiers. Tilting her chin, she asked, "And what are you going to do about those guys?"

Soeth twisted around to see two considerable northern men standing just inside the doorway. In a panic, she swiped her sword through the air, which struck no one.

"Hello, dear," Dulnear said to his wife while withdrawing his massive sword.

"I missed you," Faymia chimed.

"Give me just a second, and I will embrace you," the man from the north replied.

Then, like two wild grizzly bears tearing through a

tearoom, Dulnear and Brunnlyn separated hands, arms, and legs from the treasonous wretches.

It was not a sight for the squeamish, and Faymia found herself covering Maren's eyes. When the northerners were through, the floor was littered with living, yet severely damaged, conspirators.

>>>———·————➤

In mere moments, Faymia was in the arms of her devoted husband and Son was rushing into the room to join them. Realizing the chief was most likely in a state of shock and confusion, she began to introduce her friends. "This is my husband, Dulnear," she said.

"N-nice to meet you," Le'as blurted out, shakily extending his hand.

The man from the north sheathed his sword. Having no right hand, he reached out with his left hand in response, creating an awkward moment where he took the back of the chief's right hand and shook it heartily. "Very nice to meet you," he said, then added, "My apologies for the mess."

"And this is Son," Faymia continued, gesturing toward the boy. "He is as brave as he is handsome."

Blushing, Son stepped forward. "Pleased to meet you," he said cordially. "Your chamber is lovely," he added as his eyes swept over all of the ornate carvings.

Le'as extended his left hand this time, while Son simultaneously extended his right, creating another awkward greeting experience. This time, the chief immediately withdrew his left hand, exchanging it for his right, and the two shook hands vigorously.

Faymia suddenly realized she did not know the name of the second northerner who accompanied her friends. In a low voice she murmured to Dulnear, "And who is your friend?"

"Oh, yes," he replied. "This is my countryman, Brunnlyn. He met us on the mountain, and has been a loyal ally in our journey to join you."

"An honor," Brunnlyn said to Faymia. Turning toward Le'as, he continued, "And an honor to meet you."

With little confidence, the chief extended his right hand toward the northerner. In a clumsy motion, Brunnlyn held up his right arm, revealing that it lacked a hand. He then reached out with his left and shook the back of the chief's right hand in the same manner as Dulnear.

"Welcome," Le'as muttered. He then looked around the room and observed the brutal handiwork of the two massive men.

"Once again, I am sorry about the mess," Dulnear repeated. "It appeared you were outnumbered."

The chief sighed and shook his head. With a tired smile he said, "No apology needed. These traitors are involved in a conspiracy to bring the entire Ohdium to war." Then, as if he had forgotten for a spell, he ran over to Soeth, who had been lying on the floor next to her own severed foot. "Now, turncoat, where are Gadoar and Breag hiding?" He leveled his sword against her neck and added, "Tell me. Now!"

The guard propped herself up on her elbows, breathing heavily. Defiantly, she looked up at Le'as and answered, "Go to blazes!"

"Tell me!" the chief shouted, pressing his sword more firmly against her.

Faymia was standing near Soeth's cleaved leg. Pressing directly on the gaping wound with her foot, she said calmly, "I don't know how you became such a bitter, old spinster. I know this hurts. Now, answer your chief before I begin to scrape the mud off my boot."

Crying out in agony, Soeth screeched, "On the cliff! They're hiding amongst the damaged folk of the Ruhbrem!"

"Damaged folk?! You horrible ne'er-do-well!" Faymia yelled, and scraped her foot against the wound before lifting it off.

Soeth cried in agony and her back hit the floor, as she could no longer hold herself up. Lying there, she mumbled obscenities and threats as her trembling hands reached down in a futile gesture to ease the pain.

Le'as looked at Faymia with equal parts terror and gratitude. "We need to get both scouts, and Thuaid, to the reasoning table or I'm afraid all is lost," he explained. "But I fear we are already far too late."

"The Ruhbrem chief is a stubborn man," Faymia pointed out. "I have already begged him to parley with you, and was thrown in the dungeon for it."

"I will fetch him," Brunnlyn joined in. "Perhaps what he needs is some northern persuasion."

Dulnear laughed. "Northern persuasion. I like that. And Maren and I will fetch those two knaves from the Ruhbrem blessed village. I am sure she would be happy to identify them for me."

"Uh-huh," the young girl chirped.

"I'll stay here and help you bind these traitors," Son chimed in.

"That sounds like a great plan," Faymia agreed. Even though she wished to not be in the Ohdium, she found wonderful comfort that her friends were near. She smiled and held back a tear as she exhaled the desperation she'd held in for days.

## CHAPTER SIXTEEN
# THE PRICE OF REASON

Brunnlyn rode quickly into the Neodrec. Wasting no time with stealth or subtlety, he plowed through the crowd of contentious soldiers and stopped at the foot of the cliff dwellings. The villagers on both sides of the Rift, as well as those watching from above, froze at the sight of the large, fur-clad man. As he withdrew his sword, those nearest to him took a step back.

The man knew that stopping was a terrible idea so he remained on his horse, driving it to ascend the wooden walkway to the top. To his good fortune, the people occupying the congested path stepped aside and let him through without hesitancy. Occasionally, a child would point and ask questions about the northerner, only to be hushed by their mother or father.

When Brunnlyn reached the top he was alone, and most of the residents were turning their attention back to the ravine. He dismounted his horse and ducked into the chief's dwelling, following the directions Maren had given him.

Finally, he came upon Thuaid's chamber door. It was ajar, and he could see dim, flickering light coming from inside. Opening the door further, he could see the chief sitting at his table silently with his head in his hands.

Without breaking stride he walked behind the table, directly to Thuaid, and announced, "You are wanted at the Reonem. Come with me now or I will take you by force."

The chief looked up at the enormous man, startled by the sight of him. "W-what? Who are you?"

"It matters not," the northerner stated. "You must come now."

"But the reasoning table is on the Taalbrem side of the ravine," the man protested. "I can't go there!"

"It has been there since before there were sides," Brunnlyn argued. "Besides, if you really believed war needed to be waged, you would be down at the Neodrec ready for battle. Instead, you are hiding in your chambers, sulking like a little boy."

Thuaid's mouth dropped in indignation. He began to say something, then stopped himself. His chest filled with air, then he finally spoke. "You may be right, whoever you are. I can only assume you are in league with that one-eyed woman. However, you cannot stop what is already in motion. And doing so would only diminish the authority of my position."

"We are finished with our conversation," the northerner exclaimed matter-of-factly, and he struck the hilt of his sword against the chief's head, rendering him unconscious.

He sheathed his sword, pulled one of the beautiful tapestries down from the nearest chamber wall, and tightly rolled the chief up in it. He slung him over his shoulder and carried him out to his horse, where he secured the limp-bodied man behind his saddle. "I will never understand one's insistence on learning things the hard way," he said to himself.

Brunnlyn mounted his horse and stared over the side of the walkway. He was not looking forward to passing through the crowd with a person wrapped in a noble tapestry, and hoped his descent would be as uneventful as his arrival.

>>>————+————

As Brunnlyn's horse trotted along the walkway and down the staircases that separated each level, the experience was much like when he arrived. Villagers gawked and stepped out of the way, occasionally whispering to each other in disbelief.

When he reached the bottom of the wooden path, the crowd paid him little attention, as those closest to the Taalbrem mob were volleying insults back and forth, and the northerner wondered if they were all just waiting for their chiefs to arrive before shedding any blood.

Trying to navigate his horse through the growing, dense crowd was difficult. He came upon a cluster of men circled together as they shouted complaints and affirmations to each other about how terrible the lowground people were. One man yelled that he wished they could just get on with taking off the heads of the Taalbrem.

"Excuse me!" Brunnlyn interrupted. "I need to get through."

One of the men in the group looked up and saw the

northerner waiting on his horse. He then tapped the shoulder of the soldier standing next to him and gestured for him to step aside. The cluster of men silenced their voices and made a path.

Brunnlyn had just passed by the men when one of them cried out in dismay, "The chief! He has the chief!"

The northerner's eyes grew big and he twisted his torso to see that the rolled-up tapestry had come loose and Thuaid's entire head was exposed, bouncing against the haunches of his horse. He cursed in his native language and commanded the beast to run.

"Don't let him get away!" another man yelled, and soon the group of men was running after Brunnlyn.

Brunnlyn's lip curled and his spine stiffened as the men gave pursuit. The congested ravine made it difficult to move quickly without trampling soldiers under his oversized steed. He had now given up hope of making it through the Neodrec without calling attention to himself and pushed his way through the throngs, shouting a warning to all in his way.

Eventually, he reached the Taalbrem side, but the crowd chasing him had grown into a mob. Trumpets sounded, rocks were being thrown, and the restrained antagonizing of the villagers broke loose into mayhem.

Once the northerner reached the lowground side of the ravine, the Taalbrem soldiers mistook him for a general leading an attack, since the Ruhbrem fighters were following him, shouting and waving weapons. Now, they too were focused on stopping the humungous man.

"This is going from bad to worse!" Brunnlyn complained, and he hooked his right arm around the reins of his horse as he withdrew his sword. He swung the weapon through the air, intimidating the men around him enough to give him some space. He took the opportunity to bolt forward and took off northward through the ravine. Behind him, he could hear blades clashing and men shouting accusations at one another. It gave him an idea.

The whole point of fetching the chief was to avoid a war, not cause one. He led his horse back to the crowd. Aiming it toward the clearing behind the Taalbrem side, he shouted, "You are all miserable wretches!" As he did, the mob quieted down a bit. Continuing, he goaded, "It only took one man to capture this lousy village chief, and none of you sorry, soft baby's bottoms could stop me!"

Rumbles of indignation rose up out of the mob, which now seemed more like one army than two. "What did he just call us?!" someone bellowed.

"Baby's bottoms!" Brunnlyn reiterated. "I am taking this useless leader to the Reonem. If you want him, come and get him!" He then dashed around the crowd, took off into the woods, and didn't look back.

There was a brief moment of quiet. Then, as if the Neodrec was suddenly set on fire, the mob roared. It sounded as if every weapon was drawn and every man was fiercely focused on apprehending the northerner and claiming the chief.

---

Dulnear and Maren paused to catch their bearings. They had just traveled north to the ravine's beginning, then turned and raced up the land situated above the cliff. The place where the blessed ones lived was a small village that sat on a flat, broad clearing located a distance back from the cliff's edge.

The grass was green and lush, and a drizzling rain fell upon it. The man from the north whispered, "We must be quick. It took much longer to get here than I had anticipated."

"All right," the girl replied in a hushed tone. She had grown more and more fidgety as they approached this place, and a steady flow of nervous utterances came from her mouth as she spoke to herself quietly.

Dulnear moved his horse closer to a ring of small cottages. They were built facing each other, with their doors opening toward the center of the ring. A handful of people were visiting inside the circle, chatting cheerfully as if they were unaware of the volatile situation below. He noticed that one small child was riding the back of an adult caretaker. There was also a young man that seemed to behave much younger than he appeared. He also had a care-taker that patiently walked him across the circle to one of the houses.

"These are the blessed ones," Maren announced softly. She was sitting in front of the man from the north and turned to face him as she continued. "Le'as said I was one of them." She then turned forward again and her shoulders drooped down low.

"I see beautiful people with loving friends," Dulnear said. "There are far worse things that can be said about you than 'blessed.' " His heart grew heavy for the girl and he wanted to say more, but time was not on their side.

Maren didn't reply. Instead, she massaged her ear as she turned her attention back to the village.

The man from the north moved them forward between the two nearest cottages, getting a better look. From there, they could see even more of the circle and the people within it. He could now see that, in addition to the cottages, there was a pub, a smattering of shops, and a picnic area as well. He noticed two men sitting at a table outside of the pub. It normally would not have drawn his attention, but they seemed to be the only two able-bodied men who were not giving assistance to others who possessed challenges.

"That's them!" Maren announced. "Breag and Gadoar."

Dulnear gave his horse a kick and they jogged quickly across the circle to the pub. He dismounted his horse and stood in front of the men. "Come with me," he commanded, but they sat in their chairs, captivated by the sight of him.

Then, both of their eyes lit up and their backs stiffened as they noticed Maren sitting atop the horse. Gadoar swallowed hard and asked, "Who are you, and what's she doing here?"

Ignoring their questions, Dulnear continued. "You are ordered to come to the Reonem. Come willingly, or come by force. It makes no difference." He pulled his sword from its sheath and held it ready to strike.

"W-wait a minute," Breag protested. "What's this all about?"

"I said, now!" the man from the north boomed, and he cleaved in half the table at which they had been sitting.

The men stood up, spilling their ale on themselves,

clearly terrified by the fur-clad giant. "What's this all about? We didn't do anything!" Breag croaked.

Gadoar chimed in, "That's right. We are well-respected scouts!"

"Of opposing chiefs!" Maren shouted. "Hiding together while the entire Ohdium goes to war!"

Gadoar glared at the young girl, pointed his finger at her and began, "Listen, you little brat! You and your cyclops friend have already done enough damage!"

In the blink of an eye, Dulnear's blade swept upward, followed by the scout's freshly removed hand and a trail of blood. All was absolutely silent until the hand landed on the ground with a muffled thud.

"The woman you are referring to is my wife," the man from the north calmly explained. He then looked back at Maren and whispered, "I'm sorry you had to see that."

"No worries," Maren whispered back. "I saw what you did to Soeth."

"Right." Dulnear swallowed, then turned his attention back to the scouts.

When the two men recovered from the shock of what had just happened, they let loose screams that betrayed their cowardice, sounding like frightened children.

"My hand!" Gadoar cried out. Clutching the gushing stump, he repeated, "You cut off my hand!"

"A mere flesh wound," Dulnear consoled in a wry manner. He then sheathed his sword, grabbed the other scout's fine tunic, and tore it from his body. Handing it to the wounded Gadoar he instructed, "Here, you can dress your arm with this."

"You are absolutely mad!" Breag shouted, and he started to run away.

Dulnear quickly withdrew a knife from under his coat, flicked it through the air, and watched it become embedded in the man's left buttock, causing him to stumble to the ground. He then walked over to him and pulled the blade from his body as he screamed in pain.

Without another word, the man from the north grabbed the scout by the back of his belt, lifted him in the air, and dropped him onto the back of his horse.

"What are you doing?!" Breag bawled.

Dulnear answered with a knock to the man's head with his iron fist, causing him to lose consciousness. He then turned his attention to Gadoar, who was leaning against the tavern, white from blood loss, with a fine tunic wrapped around his arm. "Are you going to come?" he asked. "Or will I have to stab you in the buttock and knock you out too?"

The man whimpered and limped over to Dulnear's horse. "I have no place to sit," he lamented.

The man from the north smirked and replied, "Sure you do; right on top of your friend." He then hefted the scout up and laid him across the back of Breag so they were both lying on their stomachs, one on top of the other. "I will make sure you do not fall off," he added, and he took a length of rope from his saddlebag and secured the two men to the horse.

Dulnear then mounted the animal behind Maren, checked on the scouts one last time, and began to trot away from the village. As he did, he heard Maren giggling. "What are you laughing about?" he asked.

"Stab you in the buttock," the girl chuckled.

"I will let you clean the knife," the man from the north joked. And the two of them made haste to the lowground village.

## CHAPTER SEVENTEEN

# THE REONEM

F aymia stood near the Reonem, staring off toward the southern trail that led to the Taalbrem village. She felt that her idea to bring the two chiefs together was a tremendous gamble. After all, there was no guarantee the two men would behave sensibly; but it was a risk she was willing to take.

"Why are you doing this?" Le'as asked. He was seated at the reasoning table behind her, and he looked as uncertain about the plan as she did.

The woman turned toward the table and wrung her hands, allowing the question to seep in. "I really don't know," she answered honestly. "Perhaps it's because I don't want to see my birthplace turned to rubble. Or maybe I can't stand the idea of unnecessary bloodshed. Or perhaps I value justice enough to risk my life for it." She then pondered further and added, "Or it could be that I'm just not very good at letting go and walking away."

"Well," the chief replied as he stood up from his stone seat. "For what it's worth, I'm grateful you didn't. You saved my life from my mutinous guards, and hopefully the lives of everyone in the Ohdium."

Their conversation was interrupted when Son suddenly ran out to join them. "They're all tied up, and they're not happy," he announced.

"Thank you, boy," Le'as said, standing to his feet.

"It's Son," the lad said.

"Your name is Son?" the chief asked.

"Yes," the boy said cheerfully.

"Oh, I thought perhaps that was just what your friends called you," Le'as replied with an amused smile.

"Nope. That's my real name," Son said as his smile seemed to tire.

"My mistake," the chief said with a slight bow.

Then, as if catapulted from the trail itself, Brunnlyn arrived with a squirming chief on the back of his horse. "We must hurry!" he declared. "The entire Rift is in pursuit of us, and they are not far behind."

"What?" Le'as blurted. "What do you mean?"

"I mean the entire assembly from the neutral land is following me by foot," the northerner clarified. "Once they realized I was smuggling the highground chief away, they came after me."

From the back of his horse, a muffled rant could be heard from Thuaid. "Will you please get me down from here! First you concuss me with your sword, then bind me in my finest tapestry. To make matters even worse, my head bounced against the putrid haunches of your animal all the way here!"

Brunnlyn dismounted his horse, untied the knot securing the bundled man, and watched him fall to the ground. He gave a firm push with his foot, causing the chief to roll along the ground and out of the fabric that held him bound.

Thuaid scrambled to his feet, stepped sideways with a dizzy shuffle, then reached up to examine the swollen lump on his head. Clenching his jaw and pursing his lips, he hissed, "You could have been more gentle."

Maintaining a stone face, the northern warrior replied, "I am your captor, not your lover."

Snorts of suppressed laughter could be heard from the others, then Le'as stepped forward, clearing his throat. "Will you please come sit at the Reonem with me?" he pleaded. "We have much to discuss."

Thuaid glanced over at the beautifully ornate table and sighed. A look filled his eyes as if he were seeing a family member after years spent apart.

"Please," Faymia added, hoping this was the moment she'd been striving for.

Without another word, the Ruhbrem chief walked over to the reasoning table and sat across from the seat Le'as had been occupying.

>>>————•————

Faymia stood and watched the two men sitting across from each other. She realized her shoulders and neck were tensed to the point that a burning sensation was moving from the base of her skull to the middle of her back. She took a deep breath and tried to relax, but it was difficult.

Breaking the silence, Le'as said, "Please forgive me. My wicked scout was conspiring with yours to keep our people divided and fighting. To make matters worse, my personal guard was in league with them."

Thuaid swallowed hard. He glanced away for a moment, then turned his eyes back toward the lowground chief. "Do you have proof of this?" he asked.

"I do," Le'as stated. He then nodded toward Son.

Son and Faymia ran into the structure where the disloyal guard and her cohort were tied up and held in detainment. It was only seconds before the two returned, dragging a rabid, cursing Soeth, leaving her on the ground next to Thuaid. "Tell him what you told me!" Faymia commanded.

"Go to blazes!" the stubborn guard shouted.

Suddenly, Brunnlyn, who had been standing a ways off to monitor the trail leading up to the village, called out, "They are almost upon us!" Following his words, the sound of a hostile mob could be heard in the distance.

The pain in Faymia's neck was now growing unbearable. She kicked the guard in her side and demanded, "Speak!"

Soeth groaned, then began to laugh, and taunted, "It's too late. You fools deserve what you have coming to you!"

"Don't listen to her!" Faymia cried out to the highground chief. "You can still end this!"

"What happened to her foot?" Thuaid asked.

"Her overgrown donkey of a man cut it off!" the ill-tempered woman shouted.

"I gave her a tourniquet!" Son chimed in proudly.

"It was excruciating!" Soeth shouted back. "You should never be allowed near an injured person!"

Exasperated, Faymia yelled at the woman, "Tell Thuaid what you did, or I'll cut off the other foot!"

Then, like a hunted animal, Dulnear rode up from the northern prairie, only stopping once he had reached the reasoning table. He leaped from his horse and untied the two scouts, who had been thoroughly jostled from their frantic ride upon the back of his horse. "Get off my animal," he commanded, but they had already begun to roll off and onto the ground. "I'm here to deliver the refuse," he announced, then stood so they could not run away, had they the strength to do so.

When he saw Gadoar stumbling to his knees while holding his own bloody arm, Thuaid stood to his feet with his mouth agape. "So, it was all true! My mind was suspicious, but my heart refused to believe it." He then drew closer to his groveling scout and asked, "Why, lad?"

"Because I loved the silver!" Gadoar confessed. He then paused and his countenance turned cold. "I was the most honored man in the Ruhbrem. I had power that even exceeded yours. And those gullible people just lapped up every word from me without question. They deserve to die in a futile war." He then wiped his nose and began to whimper again. "Now, please, I am in great pain. Help me with my arm."

The highground chief looked sick to his stomach as he listened to the man. "Your arrogance and greed have cost us greatly." Curling his upper lip, he withdrew a dagger from his tunic and stepped closer to the sniveler. "Now, I will relieve you of your pain," he announced, plunging the blade deep into his abdomen.

Gadoar doubled over and his head fell at the chief's feet.

He wheezed and clutched his wound, then fell onto his side, dead.

Soeth and Breag looked at each other. Their eyes were wide and their skin turned pale. When Thuaid turned back to the reasoning table, they made a feeble attempt to get to their feet (or foot, in Soeth's case) but a low growl from Dulnear made them change their minds.

Taking the seat across from Le'as, Thuaid confessed, "I have been a fool. I have chosen pride over unity, and the Ohdium is poorer because of it." A tear ran down his face, getting lost in his beard. "Will you please forgive me?"

"Indeed," Le'as exclaimed as he stood from his seat.

The two men, now standing and embracing, wept together as long-lost brothers. However, their moment was shattered when Brunnlyn ran past them. There was a mob of armed villagers and soldiers close behind.

There was shouting and brandished weapons. The air was filled with aggression and rage. Suddenly, someone cried out above the clamor, "Soshayne! Soshayne!!"

A reverent silence began with those nearest to the reasoning table. An awe filled them as they witnessed the two chiefs, teary-eyed and red-nosed, speaking to each other as friends. The villagers found themselves sheathing their swords and whispering the word that meant beauty and power in unity, "Soshayne."

Faymia couldn't believe what she was seeing. The calm that had begun at the Reonem tree was now cascading back to the farthest reaches of the crowd. In the distance, she could hear a villager softly weeping. She looked in the direction of the sound and saw an old, white-haired man. He was tall and muscular, and looked oddly out of place amongst the mob.

Others soon joined the old man in his crying, and a great deal of sniffling could be heard. It was all mingled with the continuous whisper of, "Soshayne."

Thuaid and Le'as both climbed on top of the reasoning table and stood beneath the majestic, stone-carved tree. After staring out at the crowd for a moment, Thuaid addressed them. "People of the Ohdium. Today, we came within a hairsbreadth of total destruction."

Silence filled the air, and Faymia looked around her. Son was standing next to Maren near the table, and he held her hand. Dulnear was still watching over the mutinous guard and the lowground scout, who was kneeling over his coconspirator's body. Brunnlyn had joined him, and she swore she saw a tear on his cheek as he watched the two chiefs standing together.

As she looked toward the Ohdium leaders up on the table, then to her friends, and back to the chiefs, all she had endured over the past few days melted away. There came over her an awareness that what she was witnessing was historic, and she was filled with gratitude to be a part of it. She had chosen right over easy, and her choice had resulted in soshayne.

⋙ ———·——⟶

"Faymia, will you please join us here?" Le'as asked.

"M-Me?" the woman stuttered.

"Yes, come. Please," he urged.

The woman stepped up onto one of the stone seats,

then onto the table. She was nervous to join the chiefs in front of the crowd. She looked out and, from the higher vantage point, she could see that the group was much larger than she initially believed. There were people standing all the way back past the structure that contained the lowground chief's chambers.

"I would like to thank this woman who risked her life to save yours and mine," Le'as began.

"Hey, she shot me with an arrow!" someone yelled out.

"You probably had it coming!" Thuaid retorted. He then nodded toward Le'as to resume his speech.

The lowground chief paused for a moment to make sure there were no more interruptions, then continued. "Thanks to her and her young friend, a plot to pit us against each other in war was discovered. The scout Gadoar, and our scout Breag, were deliberately stoking the flames of aggression and hatred, and they were doing it for personal gain and attention."

There were whispers throughout the crowd as Le'as spoke. Villagers from both sides now gave each other apologetic glances, followed by humble nods of acknowledgement.

"I have retired our scout, Gadoar," Thuaid announced. "However, do not think this is all the sole fault of our scouts. We had a choice as to how we would respond to their reports. We could have journeyed across the Neodrec to reason together, to believe the best about each other. But we chose to accept without thinking. We chose to allow anger to sink its barbed talons into our souls and let our pride dictate our responses. I am also to blame for forsaking humility and wisdom. I even ignored warnings that could have helped us to avert many of the troubles of today. I ask that you please forgive me, and hold me accountable to use better judgement in the future."

There were audible gasps at the news of Gadoar's execution, followed by stone silence. The crowd seemed to be leaning in as the chiefs addressed them.

"I ask the same for myself too," Le'as added. "Not only was my scout involved with this treason, but my head guard as well. Thanks to the Lady Faymia and her friends, Soeth has been stopped, and will be joining Gadoar in retirement, along with my former scout, Breag."

Faymia's ears turned pink at being referred to with a noble designation. She glanced over at Dulnear. He smiled at her and mouthed, "*Lady Faymia.*"

"Today, we start anew," Thuaid declared. "We shall always strive for soshayne, regardless of the cost to pride or person. Forever forward, the people of the Ruhbrem will each year honor this day as Enheid Day. It is the day we became one people again."

"Here, here!" Le'as agreed. "As will the Taalbrem. We are all one Ohdium."

As the people applauded, Faymia made her way down off the table. When the applause subsided, a voice in the crowd began to sing a song that was known by many of them, but hadn't been sung in a generation. One voice became two, then seven, then twelve. The chiefs joined in from atop the reasoning table, and soon the entire village was engulfed in song.

Faymia looked up at the chiefs and across the crowd, then back to the table on which they stood. She did not know any of the words that were being sung, but tried to join in the chorus anyway. As she did, tears flowed, and all seemed right with the world around her.

>>> ———•———

"Once again, please forgive me for the incarceration," Thuaid apologized.

Both chiefs stood together at the table in Le'as's chamber. The crowd outside was still gathered. Some sang the old songs while others became acquainted with those who lived on the opposite side of the Ohdium.

Faymia shuffled her feet, resisting the urge to make a comment that piled more guilt onto the man. Instead, she graciously said, "All is forgiven."

"And the rest of you," the highground chief continued. He held up a goblet and addressed Son, Maren, Brunnlyn, and Dulnear. "Your ways may have been..." He cleared his throat. "Uncomfortable at the time," he murmured. He took a sip from the goblet and added, "But the right thing is seldom the easy thing, and our people are the better for it."

Le'as also raised a glass to Faymia and her friends. "Here's to the unlikeliest family I have ever met. May the Great Father smile upon you always."

"Thank you," Faymia smiled proudly.

"If you don't mind," the lowground chief continued. "I would like to make one last request."

"What can we do?" the woman asked.

"Stay," he said. "Enjoy our hospitality for a few days. You have done, and risked, so much for people you did not even know. Let us show you our appreciation."

Faymia looked at her friends standing nearby. She

wanted nothing more than to be back at Gale Hill Farm with her husband. "I came back to the place of my birth thinking it might bring me the feeling of being home," she explained. "But I realize now that I am at home when I am with them." She gripped Dulnear's hand and her eyes smiled at his. "I'm honored by your invitation, but it's time for me to return to our everyday life."

"I understand completely," Le'as said. "Just remember that you are welcome here any time. I owe you a tremendous debt of gratitude."

"As do I," Thuaid added. "The Ruhbrem are at your disposal."

"Perhaps one day we'll return for a proper holiday," Faymia nodded.

After many drawn-out hugs, awkward handshakes, kind words, and goodbyes, they parted ways. Faymia, Dulnear, Son, Maren, and Brunnlyn took to the Neodrec to recover Faymia's horse, and they rode north until they reached the road leading east to Laor.

## CHAPTER EIGHTEEN
# A GROWING CLOUD

"Now there's two of them!" someone whispered.

Faymia and her friends sat around a large, round table in the pub at Laor. They were exhausted and worn-looking. It was their final stop before arriving home at Gale Hill Farm, and they wanted to properly express their gratitude to Brunnlyn before he rejoined his Saor Brotherhood of Peaceful Warriors. However, the tavern locals seemed a bit ill at ease to see another northerner in their midst.

"Hey, I just realized that Saor rhymes with Laor," Son chirped.

"Indeed it does," Brunnlyn admitted. "However, Laor is an old southern word for inland settlement. And Saor is northern-speak for peacemaker."

"How do you know so much about languages?" the boy asked.

Answering for Brunnlyn, Dulnear broke in, "Because he had the finest teaching in Tuas-arum," he declared.

"Yes, we studied together," Brunnlyn snickered. "And I

may or may not have cheated off of Dulnear during a test or two."

"Do not give the boy ideas," Dulnear said with a wink, and they enjoyed a hearty chuckle.

Faymia enjoyed their time together but was spent. She leaned against her husband and, from time to time, would find herself closing her eyes briefly, only to be jostled back to full awareness by her company's laughter.

"Stay with us," Dulnear invited his fellow northerner. "There is a room in the cottage with Son and Maren."

Son hesitated for a moment, then added, "I suppose there is."

Brunnlyn smiled, but his eyes betrayed a concern. "I am truly honored by your invitation," he said. "But I really must return to my brethren."

Faymia felt a bit relieved by the northerner's response. She was anxious to return to her pattern of life on the farm, and company would mean more interruption to her life's rhythms—and less time with her husband.

"Am I not one of your brethren?" Dulnear asked with a smile. He then held up his right arm, exposing the metal fist Son had made for him.

Brunnlyn laughed nervously, then explained, "You are indeed the inspiration for our group. Your example has shown us a better way, without question."

Faymia was curious. Until now, she hadn't heard about the Saor, or the impact Dulnear had on them. She listened intently as the man continued.

"We have been keeping watch over you since we decided to leave Tuas-arum," he said. He then turned keenly serious. His eyes peered into Dulnear's as he continued. "All of your good deeds are coming home to roost."

Dulnear's eyes focused on the man. His chest slowly moved in and out and he quietly breathed, "What do you mean, brother?"

"In your desire to help these people, you have made enemies you cannot hope to defeat," Brunnlyn gravely warned. "The slaver king wants your head and, thanks to you, he wants the young girl returned and the boy's head as well. The blockade of madmen we experienced on the way to the Ohdium was only the beginning."

Dulnear took a deep breath and clenched his jaw. With a defiance that ran low beneath his voice he replied. "I am aware of the slaver's desire for what they call retribution."

"Are you?" Brunnlyn said. His brow pushed down upon his deep-set eyes and he leaned forward a bit more. "With tremendous respect, I must observe. We have been to your farm. We have seen your comings and goings. We knew you were in the mountains with the boy, but you never noticed us. Your senses are not as they used to be, and I fear your skills may have become dull."

Faymia braced herself inwardly. She was well aware of the northern-folk's reputation for flaring tempers. A direct criticism like the one Dulnear had just received could end in swordplay.

Instead, the man exhaled and looked away. Then, bringing his eyes back upon Brunnlyn, he said, "Thank you. Perhaps it is time I sharpen my abilities and, while I am at it, accelerate the boy's training."

"You speak wisdom, my friend," Brunnlyn said. He leaned back a bit and raised one eyebrow as he continued.

"Dark clouds are coming. If you plan to run, then do so immediately. If you plan to make a stand at Gale Hill, then I suggest you not wait to fortify your home."

"Mayeth agat," Dulnear said grimly. It was a northern phrase that roughly implied fighting to the death in order to defend those dearest to you.

"Mayeth agat," Brunnlyn replied.

Faymia's fatigue seemed to dissipate as she heard the two men speak. She had known for some time that the words they spoke were a probability, but had put it out of her mind. Now the roadblock she had encountered a few days ago made sense to her, and a feeling of foreboding settled upon her.

The five travelers stood outside the pub at Laor, bellies full and bodies weary. There was just enough daylight for Faymia and her friends to make it home before dark, if they hurried.

"Again, many thanks for your aid," Dulnear said as he placed his hand upon his countryman's shoulder.

Brunnlyn returned the gesture and nodded, "It is my honor."

"Will we see you again?" Son asked.

Brunnlyn crouched down so he could be eye to eye with the boy. "If you are fortunate, you will not anytime soon," he said. "But I and my brethren will be there should the need arise." He then looked over at Maren and added, "Take good care of her. Her heart is great."

"Goodbye," the young girl chirped, taking a small step

toward the horses and motioning that she would like to get on one.

"Thank you again," Faymia added, feeling almost as impatient as Maren, but keeping those feelings hidden.

"Goodbye, my lady," the northerner said with a hint of a bow.

They mounted their horses and rode them slowly out to the road. After a little more small talk, they aimed their steeds in opposite directions.

"Goodbye, Brunnlyn," Son said with a tired smile. Maren was perched on the boy's horse as well and she waved at the northerner.

"Keep training, lad," the man answered. "I see something great in you." He then kicked the sides of his horse, driving the animal east, down the road.

When Brunnlyn was further away, Faymia set her red, achy eye on Dulnear. "Let's go home, my Layoak," she said.

"Let us," her husband responded.

And the four of them returned home to Gale Hill Farm.

>>>———·———

Mist covered the ground, and the morning air was still and quiet. Crouching behind a low-lying shrub, Faymia eyed a great elk down the shaft of her arrow. Her arm was like steel as it held back the tension of her bow. She was dreaming of hunting, as she often did. Only this time, the dream did not carry the usual sense of freedom and confidence these unconscious outings usually offered.

A feeling of foreboding filled her, and she could feel the

dark shadow of another covering her back. She re-quivered her arrow and spun around. There, standing before her, was Tcharron, her former slave owner. His clothing and dark, well-kept hair and beard were just as she remembered. But the usual smell of expensive cologne was replaced by the reek of death, and dried blood drenched his neck and torso.

Startled, Faymia gasped, "You're dead! How can you be here?"

"Indeed I am," Tcharron replied. As he took a deep breath, fresh blood began to ooze from the many puncture wounds throughout his chest. "If I had known this would be my fate, I would not have helped you and your friends."

"I'm sorry," the woman whispered. She could feel regret and anger radiate from the man in front of her. She wanted to run, but something held her feet motionless.

"I'm sure," the man replied, half rolling his eyes.

"If it is any comfort, we were able to find our young Maren, and we brought her home," Faymia explained.

"I know," Tcharron rasped, and an icy expression formed across his face. "I've come to warn you."

Faymia knew exactly what the man was going to warn her about, for Brunnlyn's words had not left her mind since they had departed.

"Ocmallum is coming," the specter warned. "I don't know how a ragamuffin boy, a one-handed northerner, a little girl, and a used-up slave managed to do it. You have made enemies with the most powerful slaver in Aun, and he plans to spare no resource to see you all suffer greatly before ending your lives."

Faymia's hands began to tremble. The world around them seemed to disintegrate and drift away. As it did, fear and weakness replaced that world. She closed her eyes for a moment and whispered a prayer, drawing on strength from the Great Father. "Sometimes, doing what's right has its consequences," she declared. "And we will face them together the best we can."

Tcharron gave a crooked grin from purple lips and pale, dead skin. He then looked over the woman from head to toe, noticing. "There's something different about you."

"What do you mean?" she asked.

The man sniffed the air and observed, "There is steel in your soul. That's good. You're going to need it. But there's something else."

"Something else?"

Tcharron's face relaxed and the smell of decay seemed to fade away. Tilting his head, he murmured, "It's power." Then, squinting as if in thought, he added, "And beauty."

Immediately, the sound of the old woman's voice from the Ruhbrem filled Faymia's mind. The memory of the past few days crashed over her like a frigid wave. As it did, she closed her eyes once more. When she opened them, Tcharron was gone, and she was standing in the field behind low-lying shrubs once more.

***

Faymia opened her eyes to see her husband lying beside her in their bed. His eyes were open and he appeared lost in thought as he stared at the ceiling. When she turned her body to face his, he looked her way.

"Good morning," Dulnear murmured sleepily.

Faymia examined his face, tracing each line along his

forehead with her eyes. "What troubles you, my love?" she asked.

Dulnear turned on his side as well, facing her completely. "You spoke in your sleep."

Somewhat embarrassed, the woman apologized, "I'm sorry. I didn't mean to wake you."

"No apology necessary," the man from the north said. "Even in your dreams, you speak wisdom. I think we are all finding peace to be elusive in the shadow of Ocmallum's threat."

"Maybe we should run," Faymia suggested, though her heart did not believe it was the wisest course of action.

"Perhaps," Dulnear sighed. "But living the rest of our lives looking over our shoulders would be a cruel way to spend our days."

The pale morning light washed over their room with a cheerless gray. The woman turned onto her back and stared out their window into the endless, white sky. Thinking out loud, she asked, "What if we return to Tuasarum?"

Scratching his chin, Dulnear replied, "Indeed, we may be able to buy some time there. But the slave king has northerners in his employ. They would eventually find us."

A tear began to run down Faymia's face. For her entire existence, she had longed for the life she was now living. In her wildest dreams, she couldn't believe she would marry a man as loving and strong as Dulnear. She deeply loved Son and Maren, and treasured each day on Gale Hill. Without realizing that she was speaking out loud, she observed, "It's worth fighting for."

The man from the north wiped away the tear that was

traveling along his wife's face. "Do you mean to say you prefer to stay and fight?"

"Yes," she answered. "Our life together here is more than I could have imagined. It's worth fighting for." Another tear fell from her eye as she turned face-to-face with her husband once again.

Dulnear gently ran his finger over the scar that ran from her blind eye. With a deep sigh, he said, "You have so much fight in you. It is one of my favorite qualities. I agree whole-heartedly that what we have here is worth the clashing of swords and spilling of blood. But, is it worth dying for?"

"Oh, my husband," the woman sniffed. "You have set me free in more ways than you will ever know. If we run, my life would once again be ruled by the whims of slavers. For, like you said, we would be exchanging our freedom for a life under constant threat and paranoia. We would forever be running and preparing for a doom that may or may not find us. Yes, I would rather die than half-live my days."

Staring deeply into Faymia's face, Dulnear's chin began to quiver as he answered, "Then I will stand by your side and fight with you until the end. I only request one thing."

"What is that?" the woman asked.

"That we speak to Son and Maren and give them a choice. They may want to leave, and I would not fault them for it."

"I understand," the woman replied. She embraced her husband as they shed another tear together.

They lay there until the sky was a bit brighter, then prepared to walk up to Son and Maren's cottage.

"I'm going to step outside!" Faymia called from the kitchen. She had finished a small breakfast and was anxious to leave and speak to Son and Maren about their plans.

Dulnear, who was in the other room slipping on his boots, called back, "Go ahead, my love. I will join you posthaste."

When the woman stepped out the door, she was greeted with a ghastly odor. "Oohf!" she coughed. "What is that smell?"

Just a few paces in front of her, she saw an enormous, cat-like creature curled on the ground, sleeping. Its ears twitched and it sprang to its feet.

"Dulnear!" Faymia cried out as she withdrew a dagger from her tunic.

The man from the north sprinted out the door. Seeing the beast, he shouted, "Verrox!"

Immediately, the kottur sprinted over to the man and began licking his beard.

"What is that thing?" Faymia demanded.

"Oh, a friend I made on our way to the Ohdium," he said. He then told her about how they had helped the animal and it had returned the favor, leaving out the part about it nearly killing Son.

"Well, your friend stinks!" she exclaimed, curling her nose upward.

"Do not be rude," Dulnear admonished. "She will not hurt you. I think she feels indebted to me. Here, give her a little scratch behind the ears."

Faymia tentatively reached up and scratched the kottur's head. As she did, the beast dragged its course tongue across her face. "It's like having a dead fish dragged across my cheek!" she gagged.

"There, see? She likes you," the man from the north beamed.

"Well then, I guess we have a pet," the woman sighed, trying to wipe the odor from her face.

The massive beast followed as the two of them walked up to Son and Maren's cottage, preparing themselves for a discussion they wished they did not need to have.

I hope you enjoyed reading *Hunter From the Rift*. Its characters and their adventures are near and dear to me. If you would like information about the next book in the Aun series, as well as other forthcoming projects, please visit my website, www.leebezotte.com and sign up for my e-newsletter. You can also join me on Facebook and Twitter.

Thank you for journeying with me!

Lee Bezotte

www.ingramcontent.com/pod-product-compliance
Lightning Source LLC
Chambersburg PA
CBHW030348200626
46808CB00022B/619